"Are You Still Willing To Be My Surrogate?" Colt Asked.

He reached for her hair again. The fire-lit strands slipped through his fingers like ribbons of silk.

"Yes." Melanie's breathless voice sent a surge of sensual heat coursing through his veins.

Colt shuddered. He wouldn't permit this to happen. He wouldn't confuse his need for a child with desire for the woman willing to carry it. That's what was happening, he told himself. He was vulnerable and so was she. Their physical compulsion to produce a baby was creating false intimacy. His urge to taste her citrus-scented skin and run his hands through her thick, autumn hair would go away once his seed was planted.

Wouldn't it?

Dear Reader,

Welcome to Silhouette Desire—where you're guaranteed powerful, passionate and provocative love stories that feature rugged heroes and spirited heroines who experience the full emotional intensity of falling in love!

This October you'll love our new MAN OF THE MONTH title by Barbara Boswell, *Forever Flint*. Opposites attract when a city girl becomes the pregnant bride of a millionaire outdoorsman.

Be sure to "rope in" the next installment of the exciting Desire miniseries TEXAS CATTLEMAN'S CLUB with *Billionaire Bridegroom* by Peggy Moreland. When cattle baron Forrest Cunningham wants to wed childhood friend Becky Sullivan, she puts his love to an unexpected test.

The always-wonderful Jennifer Greene returns to Desire with her magical series HAPPILY EVER AFTER. *Kiss Your Prince Charming* is a modern fairy tale starring an unforgettable "frog prince." In a sexy battle-of-the-sexes tale, Lass Small offers you *The Catch of Texas*. Anne Eames continues her popular miniseries MONTANA MALONES with *The Unknown Malone*. And Sheri WhiteFeather makes her explosive Desire debut with *Warrior's Baby*, a story of surrogate motherhood with a twist.

Next month, you'll really feel the power of the passion when you see our new provocative cover design. Underneath our new covers, you will still find six exhilarating journeys into the seductive world of romance, with a guaranteed happy ending!

Enjoy!

Joan Marlow Golan
Senior Editor, Silhouette Desire

Please address questions and book requests to:
Silhouette Reader Service
U.S.: 3010 Walden Ave., P.O. Box 1325, Buffalo, NY 14269
Canadian: P.O. Box 609, Fort Erie, Ont. L2A 5X3

WARRIOR'S BABY
SHERI WHITEFEATHER

SILHOUETTE *Desire*®

Published by Silhouette Books

America's Publisher of Contemporary Romance

SILHOUETTE BOOKS

ISBN 0-373-76248-8

WARRIOR'S BABY

Copyright © 1999 by Sheree Henry-WhiteFeather

Visit us at www.romance.net

Printed in U.S.A.

SHERI WHITEFEATHER

lives in Southern California and enjoys ethnic dining, summer powwows and visiting art galleries and vintage clothing stores near the beach. Since her one true passion is writing, she is thrilled to be a part of the Silhouette Desire line. When she isn't writing, she often reads until the wee hours of the morning.

Sheri also works as a leather artisan with her Native American husband, Dru. They have one son and a menagerie of pets, including a pampered English bulldog and four equally spoiled Bengal cats. She would love to hear from her readers. You may write to her at: P.O. Box 5130, Orange, California 92863-5130.

To Dru and Nikki WhiteFeather for the beauty in my life,
to my mom and two dads for always believing in me, my
sister Elaine for heartfelt prayers and my in-laws for
sharing their heritage. A very special thanks to
Judy Duarte and Chris Green for being the most
dedicated critique partners in the world, and to
Maureen Child for her honesty and advice. Another
sincere thanks to Irene Goodman, Melissa Jeglinski
and Joan Marlow Golan, the hardworking professionals
who made this book happen. All of you have contributed
to the dream.

One

Melanie Richards had to do it.

Now.

As she strode onto the balcony, the sea breeze lifted her fire-tinted locks and billowed her loose cotton skirt. She slid onto a rattan chair, tucked her legs beneath her and stared at the cordless telephone.

How many times today had she chickened out? Five? Six? She'd lost count.

She gazed at the glass tabletop where the torn scrap of paper beside her coffee cup rippled in the wind, seven digits and an area code in danger of being whisked away.

She swiped the phone and began punching buttons. She didn't need the number. She had memorized it.

The long-distance rings sounded in her ear. One...two... three...

A man answered. "Hello?"

Oh, God. The husky drawl was rich and smooth.

"Is this Colt Raintree?" She knew it was. Tall, broad-shouldered, black-haired Colt, a man as fast and dangerous as the single-action revolver he had been named after.

"Yes."

"Hi, this is—" *Gertrude. Geeky Gertie. The other teenagers used to call me that. Remember? You never did, though. You were sympathetic and kind.* "Melanie Richards."

"Do I know you?"

Yes, but it's been thirteen years. I use my middle name now and look different. You wouldn't recognize me. "No. Gloria Carnegie told me you were hiring a surrogate, and I—"

He interrupted, his tone edged with suspicion. "Fred's wife?"

"Yes. Gloria's a patient of Dr. Miller and just happened to hear about your situation. She contacted me because she thought I might be interested in helping you out." Melanie paused and gulped a breath of salty air, her heart threatening to beat its way out of her chest. "And I am, but I've never done anything like this before."

His voice softened, just a little. "I'd prefer to discuss this in person. Are you free tomorrow?"

She gazed out at the ocean. As dusk settled over a summer sky, streaks of mauve painted a foaming wave as it crashed onto the shore. A pair of seagulls frolicked in the swell, dipping and gliding. *Did you know that I was in love with you?*

"I can't meet with you that soon. You see, I live in California," she said, then added quickly, "but I'm coming to Montana next week."

He heaved a sigh and she imagined him raking his hands through his hair. Such beautiful hair. Thick and shiny.

"I suppose next week would be all right. We could meet at the Steer House. Are you familiar with it?"

"Yes." She had eaten at the Steer House many times. Mountain Bluff didn't have many restaurants. "Any day you choose is fine." Her only other commitment was visiting with Gloria.

"How about Wednesday? We can discuss the details over lunch," he offered, sounding more reserved than she remembered.

But then why shouldn't he? To him Melanie Richards was a stranger, a woman who lived over nine hundred miles away.

"All right. I'll call you to confirm."

"Fine." Colt ended the conversation politely. "It was nice talking to you but I have to go."

They exchanged proper goodbyes. The receiver went dead.

On the following Wednesday, Melanie arrived at the Steer House wearing a simple black dress, a linen blazer and understated jewelry. Her freshly-washed hair fell freely about her shoulders.

Within minutes she was seated at a candle-lit table where she was left to wait for Colt.

Melanie was accustomed to business meetings. Luncheons, dinners. She always wore black, arrived early, ordered a light meal and smiled charmingly. She had it down pat. Today, of course, was different. She wasn't in L.A., selling a chic artistic design. This was her hometown and the cowboy due to arrive wouldn't be interested in seeing her portfolio. In fact, she had no idea what Colt Raintree would be interested in seeing. She'd never been considered for motherhood before.

When she looked up, her heart leaped into her throat. Tall and strong and more handsome than she remembered, Colt strode behind the hostess. When the girl stopped and Colt moved forward, Melanie feasted her eyes.

His slim-fitting jeans looked new. A fancy black-and-white shirt, combining embroidery and a western yoke, stretched the boundaries of his broad shoulders. Long black hair, secured at his nape, boasted his heritage. Colt had always reminded her of a jungle cat, sleek and muscular with exotic-shaped eyes and a raw sensuality of which he seemed unaware.

He slid into a chair across from Melanie and smiled politely. Neither spoke until the hostess departed.

He reached across the table to extend his hand. The flickering candle shadowed the sharp angle of his cheekbones. He had aged well. The lithe, rakish boy had grown into a warrior. Dark eyes revealed masculine depth.

"Melanie, right?"

She nodded and accepted his hand. It was big, callused and warm. His touch spread through her like an ache. She still loved him. Not just the memory, but the man. She believed in second chances. This was hers.

"Nice to meet you. I'm Colt."

Hands separating, their gazes locked. "Am I late?" he asked.

"No." She smiled. "I was early."

Apparently he didn't recognize her, but then she hadn't really expected him to. She bore little resemblance to the timid girl he had known so long ago. During her third year in California, she'd been struck by a car. The near-fatal car accident had resulted in a necessary surgical procedure. One that had altered her features.

The busboy reappeared with another glass of water. Colt opened the menu. "Do you want to decide on lunch first?"

"Sure." Although too nervous to be hungry, when the waitress arrived, she ordered broiled chicken.

Colt decided on the steak and scampi special. Both chose salad over soup. They muddled through small talk: the weather, the Western artifacts in the restaurant. She waited for him to get down to business. He did, right after their salads were delivered.

"You're not what I expected," he said. "I pictured someone, I don't know, more momish."

She had no idea what his concept of momish was. "Like a fifties television mom?"

"Yeah, something like that." He grinned. The same, slow dangerous grin that had melted her heart thirteen years ago. When it faded, a muscle in his jaw twitched. "Some of the women I've met with haven't liked the idea that I'm single. How do you feel about that?"

Her stomach constricted. The interview had begun. "I can't very well hold that against you. I'm not married, either."

He reached for the bread basket. "No boyfriend to consult?"

She moved the lettuce around on her plate. "No. There's no one."

Colt tore a roll in half and buttered the center. "We need to be straight with each other. You tell me why you're willing to be a surrogate and I'll tell you why I'm looking for one."

The table was fairly secluded, for which she was grateful. She certainly didn't want the other patrons to get an earful. She'd been rehearsing her speech all day. Being straight was out of the question. She'd have to combine bits of the truth with some creative story telling. California BS, she called it. Embellish your assets. Tell the client what they want to hear.

She started with the truth. "I'm a foster child. Consequently, I've learned to make my own way. When we were kids, Gloria and I lived next door to each other. We were best friends. As you know, she's the one who mentioned your situation to me. The idea of a single man wanting a child so much fascinated me. That's why I contacted you." She sipped her water, then continued. She had Colt's undivided attention, something she'd always longed for. "I don't believe I could carry a child for a couple. I wouldn't be comfortable being impregnated by another woman's husband."

He seemed mildly satisfied. "Do you have any children?"

Melanie shook her head. "I've been too busy with my career. I'm an illustrator. I've designed just about everything. Greeting cards, posters, calendars, book covers. There hasn't been much time for anything else."

He pushed his half-eaten salad away and leaned forward, dark eyes probing. "You don't look familiar."

Her pulse raced. "Should I?"

"You said you were Gloria's neighbor. That's means you grew up around here."

He studied her carefully. She thought he liked what he saw. Melanie recognized masculine admiration. She'd worked hard to achieve it: a strenuous daily workout, hair tinting, a carefully chosen wardrobe and just the right amount of makeup.

"Do you remember Gloria?" she asked. Colt wouldn't have known that Gertrude had been friends with Gloria. The two had never been in his company together.

"Sure," he answered. "I used to see her around. I went to high school with Fred. They were sweethearts."

She smirked and raised a brow. "I went to Saint Theresa's. I was a *good* girl."

"Oh, yeah?" He laughed. "Well, I was probably the baddest boy in town. Lucky for you we never met."

He was still grinning like a rogue when the waitress brought their meals. He cut into his meat. She studied the silverware pattern and pushed away her guilt. She wanted to be someone new in his eyes.

She glanced up and met his amused gaze. "Your reputation precedes you, Colt. I know all about you."

His smile disappeared. "Everything?"

She wasn't sure what *everything* was. "Just gossip, I suppose. People like to talk."

He reached for his water. "The gossip started with my mom. Her folks, my grandparents, built Bluff Creek, the recreational ranch I inherited. Grandma ran the bed and breakfast and Grandpa took tourists on pack rides. Fishing and camping, nature trails, that sort of thing." A short laugh barked from his chest. "But when Grandpa hired this big Indian fellow to help out, he got a little more than he bargained for. Toby Raintree took a shine to my mom. Problem was, she was only sixteen and Toby was twenty or so. Grandpa sent the Cheyenne packing, but the damage had already been done. I arrived nine months later."

Colt raked his hands through his hair, deep-set eyes reflecting old wounds. Melanie thought about her own unbecoming beginnings. She was illegitimate, too. "You don't have to tell me everything, Colt. If it makes you uncomfortable…"

"We're talking about making a baby. I think we should be candid with each other." A shrug jerked his brawny shoulders. "Besides, my family loved me, even if I had a bit of Toby in me. I wasn't wild on purpose. I wasn't trying to prove anything. It's just who I was."

She teased him with a feminine toss of her head. He was staring. Seriously considering her for the baby-making job, she thought. "I heard you were a spoiled rich boy."

His grin was wry. "Overindulged, maybe."

The waitress came by and cleared their plates. He had finished his meal, she'd done a lot of rearranging on her plate. If he noticed her lack of appetite, he didn't comment on it. They both ordered a cup of coffee, passed on dessert.

"I have to know, Melanie. Is it the money?"

She couldn't help herself from bristling. "I didn't bring up your family's money because I need it."

"It's my money now. My family's gone. And I'm offering a fair amount to the woman who has my baby. I have a right to know what your true motivation is."

She wanted to leap across the table, pummel his chest and shout that she loved him, that she hoped to keep his baby and share a life with him. "I plan to give the money to charity. A children's organization of some kind. I have a successful career. I'm not in the business of selling babies."

"And I'm not in the business of buying them," he retorted, then softened his tone. "I had a daughter…a sweet little girl…" His eyes turned watery. "God, it seems like a lifetime ago. I just miss being a father. I didn't mean to offend you. What you do with the money is your prerogative."

He reached across the table for her hand, squeezed it apologetically. "Are you still interested, or did I just prove what an idiot I can be?"

Longing made her voice breathless. "I'm still interested."

His fingertips brushed hers. "Will you come by the ranch tomorrow? I'd like to show you around. It's a great place for a kid to grow up."

"Certainly. I'd love to."

Two hours later Melanie rocked on Gloria's weather-beaten porch, wearing a red cotton blouse, faded blue jeans, Harley-Davidson boots and an anxious expression that mirrored her fluttering heart.

Gloria's youngest hummed a contented tune. The towheaded four-year-old reached for his favorite toy, a yellow dump trunk packed with tiny stones from the freshly graveled driveway. When he grinned, the cherry Popsicle stain around his mouth widened.

Seated beside him on the front step, his mother touched the back of his head and shuddered. "Colt's daughter was about Joey's age when she died. I can't imagine losing a child."

Melanie stilled the bentwood rocker. She remembered that summer. She'd come home for one of Gloria's baby showers and learned Colt had just buried his estranged wife and daughter.

As usual, he'd been the talk of the town. She'd heard he was inconsolable, shutting out the world around him.

"What do you really think about him looking for a surrogate?"

"Truthfully?" Gloria ruffled her cropped hair, the spiky strawberry-blond strands still damp from Joey's swimming lessons. She had always been fresh-scrubbed looking with a generous supply of freckles, cosmetics low on her list of priorities. "I think he's lonely and misguided. He should marry again and have children the traditional way."

"I had lunch with him today." Melanie set the rocker in motion. It felt good to breathe the clean Montana air. Almost as life-sustaining as the sound of Colt's husky drawl.

"A date? Oh, Mel, that's wonderful."

She gnawed her bottom lip. "It wasn't exactly a date. I didn't tell him my name used to be Gertrude. You see, we weren't really meeting for old time's sake."

Joey's mother shooed him into the house, bribing him with another Popsicle. "Just one," she cautioned as the boy forgot about the truck and dashed off. She turned to Melanie, one eyebrow arching. "What's going on?"

Melanie gazed out at the front yard. Along the fence, rows of late-blooming flowers and tall, scattered weeds fought for control. The garden hose attached to a sprinkler head slithered across the overgrown lawn like a giant snake. In the center of the damp grass a proud tree yielded a makeshift swing, a big, black tire swaying in the breeze.

Her beachfront property paled by comparison. A happy home surpassed a lonely, upscale, condo any day. "I told him I was interested in being his surrogate."

"Oh, my Lord! You didn't!"

Melanie set her jaw. "I did. And I am."

Gloria shook her cropped head. "You, my dear, are not a good candidate. You've never even had a child. You'd never be able to turn your baby over to him."

Plastering a smile on her face, Melanie ignored the other woman's disapproving scowl. "Yes, I could. I'm too wrapped up in my career to think about raising a child. I'm—"

"Lying," Gloria provided.

The phony smile faded. "You said it yourself. Colt needs a wife."

"But he doesn't want a wife. He wants a child, no strings attached."

"I'll make him change his mind." That car accident had given her a new outlook on life. It had taught her to go after what she wanted. And more than anything, she wanted Colt.

When Gloria's expression reflected Melanie's biggest fear, her confidence wavered. Reminding herself to breathe, she closed her eyes and said a silent prayer. *Please God, make Colt want me, too. Don't let me fail.*

She opened her eyes and addressed her friend. "You're the one who gave me this idea."

"What are you talking about?"

Melanie took another deep breath. How typical of Gloria to act innocent. "You couldn't wait to tell me that he was looking for a surrogate. And you even said that I should be the one to have his baby."

Gloria wrung her hands together. "I was kidding."

"Baloney, that was a subliminal message and you darn well know it."

"Sublimi—" The other woman stood up and began to pace. "Oh, my Lord, what have I done?"

Melanie forced a grin. If she couldn't convince Gloria, then how could she convince Colt? "Oh, quit fretting. A little subconscious matchmaking never hurt anyone. Just wish me luck. Support my decision."

The other woman paused. "Are you sure you're in love with Colt? True love happens over time, and the two of you have never really spent any time together. I want you to be certain before you—"

"I am," Melanie professed adamantly, meeting her friend's concerned gaze. "From the first moment I saw him, I knew he was meant to be part of my life. And we did spend time together—every weekend for almost two years—I rode at his family's ranch. He was good to me, Gloria. The kindest person I'd ever known."

"He may not be so kind once he finds out what you're up to." When Gloria paced again, the wood planks squeaked below her feet. "I hate to say this, but there is the possibility he might not fall in love with you. Think about how serious this is, Mel."

"I have." *Long and hard, every waking moment.* "I'm not trying to trick Colt. And I know what the consequences are. If he doesn't fall in love with me, then I'll honor our original agreement." Deep down, she kept telling herself that wouldn't happen, but the realist in her knew it could.

Gloria's jaw dropped. "You'd give him the baby?"

"Yes." The next breath she took hurt. Deeply. "I vowed a long time ago that if I could ever repay Colt for his kindness, I would. I've always wanted to change his life the way he changed mine." She set the rocker in motion again—a movement as gentle as the breeze, as tender as Colt's heart. "He made me realize my worth, helped me to believe in myself. I'm successful and strong because he convinced me I could be.

"So you see, Gloria. If I have to, I'll give him our baby." She would give Colt a part of her that would live forever. "But as I said before, I'll do whatever I can to make him want me."

The other woman's expression softened. "Oh, Mel, you really do love him."

"Yes. I always have." Melanie recalled how sensitive and protective he had been. When the other teenagers who frequented the rental stables made leering cracks about what a "nerdy brain" she was, Colt had countered their attacks, professing "I think intelligent women are sexy." Time and time again, Colt Raintree had been her champion, her knight in shining armor. He would touch her cheek and tell her she was perfect—sweet and pure—one of earth's angels.

Although their lives had taken separate paths, Colt's image had never been far from her heart. She wanted him to be her first love. Her only love.

As an image of her teenage self surfaced, Melanie's stomach fluttered. What an image: a shy, skinny little girl with mousy brown hair and a mouthful of silver braces. "Colt didn't recognize me."

"How could he? Let's face it, you've changed." Gloria tilted her blond head. "You do plan on telling him who you are, right?"

"Yes, but not right away." Colt wanted a professional relationship with his surrogate. A woman who adored him during their teenage years certainly didn't fall into that category. Until his baby lay cradled in her womb, she would keep her identity a secret.

"Are you sure that's wise? I mean—" Gloria paused as Joey scampered out the front door and down the rickety porch steps. The boy had a Popsicle, probably his fourth, the rainbow around his mouth a conspicuous giveaway.

His mother latched on to his shirttail. "How many of those have you had?"

He squirmed. "Two."

"Joey?"

"Three."

She released her hold. "No more, okay?"

He grinned. His teeth were blue. "Okay, Mom."

The child leaped onto the wet grass and both women laughed. *Mom.* Just the word alone made Melanie's womb ache. The only man she had ever dreamed of having a baby with was Colt. At this point, being inseminated with his seed sounded romantic.

Melanie Richards had built a successful career, acquired self-esteem and survived a near-fatal accident, yet she had never forgotten the wild, black-haired boy who had treated her kindly when others had not; the boy with whom she had fallen hopelessly in love.

Colt wondered if she'd be early. They had agreed on 10:00 a.m. He glanced at his watch. It was 9:33.

Melanie Richards was an enigma. A beautiful, single, successful lady willing to have a baby for someone else. Something didn't add up. Maybe she needed the dough. He wasn't quite buying her I-plan-to-give-the-money-to-charity story. Being a surrogate was a job—nine months out of a woman's life. He didn't begrudge paying for the service, yet the idea of buying his own baby, in a sense, left him cold. He wanted the perfect scenario, a woman who needed to give a child as much as he needed to receive one. Melanie was going to have to tell him straight out why she was offering him the ultimate sacrifice. The most precious of gifts. Her motivation was still vague.

Colt flipped his leg over the leather recliner and reached for the coffee mug. Dang, he was actually anxious about seeing her again. Unfortunately he found himself physically attracted to her: a youthful complexion, big cornflower blue eyes, shoulder-length hair the color of autumn leaves, each strand unique in its vibrance. And her body? Enticing curves a man could ride, slow and sensual, like a smooth hypnotic current.

He jerked forward when the doorbell sounded, locking the recliner in place. It was 9:40. She was early.

He pulled open the door. Pushed away his lust. Business and pleasure didn't mix where women were concerned.

"Hi." She smiled. She looked younger than the day before. Her blue jeans were faded, fraying at the knees, her denim blouse tied at the waist. A green ribbon secured her ponytail, but wispy tendrils had worked loose, gently framing a heart-shaped face. She smelled like citrus-scented soap, clean and fresh.

Colt glanced down and let out a low whistle. Her Western boots were ostrich. The lady had class. Money.

He stepped away from the door. "Come in."

She was still smiling. "Boots are my weakness."

Women like you are mine, he wanted to say. "Yeah, I can see that."

She gazed around the room. "Impressive place."

He followed the line of her eyes and assessed his surroundings with renewed interest. Constructed of native timber and pegged-beam ceilings, the six-bedroom homestead used to serve as the main lodge. He'd considered renting it out and moving into one of the log cabins out back, but couldn't bring himself to abandon his daughter's room. Her pink canopy bed and favorite stuffed animals remained there, waiting for a child who would never return.

"Big place for one guy, huh?" he asked.

"Soon there will be two of you."

He smiled at the thought. His home had been empty far too long. "The patter of little feet."

"Little boots," she amended.

He winked at her, something he hadn't done to a woman in a long time. Melanie reminded him of his youth for some reason, and although she didn't look familiar, she felt familiar. Something he didn't quite understand. "Do you want a cup of coffee or iced tea or something?"

"Tea sounds nice."

She followed him into the kitchen then sat down at the oak table in the adjoining dining room. It seated twelve. He poured a tall glass of sun tea and joined her. "We used to have people around all the time. Tourists. Sometimes I hated it, having strangers in my house. Other times, I really enjoyed it. When my grandparents died, I couldn't keep the bed and breakfast going. I raise quarter horses. That keeps me busy."

"My work keeps me busy, too."

He brushed his hair out of his eyes. "If we decide to go through with this, I want full custody of the child. I'd want this to be like an adoption on your part."

She gazed into her tea. "I know."

"I couldn't take another custody battle, Melanie. You have to be sure you can do this. You have to convince me I can trust you, that you're being completely honest."

A shadow hooded her blue eyes. They went from daylight to dark in an instant. "A custody battle? I don't understand."

He blew an anxious breath. His scars hadn't healed. Dredging up the past hurt, but she had a right to know. "I wasn't happily married. I married Shelly because of the baby. I never loved her the way a husband should. We argued all the time. She kept accusing me of cheating. I hadn't been, but she was obsessively jealous. I couldn't even talk to another woman. After a few miserable years, I told her I couldn't take it anymore, that I wanted a divorce."

Melanie twisted the dainty gold chain around her neck. Colt studied her nervous fingers, bit the inside of his lip and continued. "Things got real ugly after that. And Meagan, our daughter, got caught in the middle." He tugged a hand through his hair.

"We ended up in court. It was a long, drawn-out process, but eventually I got custody of Meagan. Shelly was issued weekend and holiday visitations. The psychiatrist who testified seemed to think it was in our daughter's best interest to remain with me."

He pushed his chair back and gripped the tabletop, expelling pain and frustration from the past. "But the court ruling didn't mean a damn thing because the first weekend Shelly had Meagan, she closed her bank accounts and ran. She kidnapped my little girl. Took her away from me."

His brown knuckles whitened. The worst was yet to come. "Even though I searched and hired people, we never found them. A whole year went by and then one day the police showed up at my door. Shelly and Meagan had been killed in a drive-by shooting in Chicago." Colt caught his breath, felt the familiar sting beneath his eyes. "The last time I saw my five-year-old daughter was at her funeral."

Someone had killed an innocent child because they'd mistaken Shelly's car for one belonging to a rival gang member. His baby girl had met a violent death on a cold, empty street. Oh, they'd caught the lone gunman, but knowing that bastard was rotting in jail hadn't eased his pain. Colt had vowed to himself over and over that no one would ever take another child from him again. Not the child's mother nor some sick, violent stranger. He would protect this baby with his life.

Melanie looked up. Her eyes were lined with tears. "I'm sorry," she whispered.

Colt's heart clenched. A part of him hated what he was asking her to do. Deep down, he knew a child should be raised by two loving parents, yet Shelly's deception had made it impossible for him to welcome another woman back into his life. Had Shelly not kidnapped Meagan, his daughter would still be alive.

He trapped Melanie's gaze. Finding a surrogate mother was his only recourse.

"If we create a child, are you willing to hand the baby over to me, walk away and not look back?"

Colt waited. Melanie Richards didn't respond.

Two

"Melanie?"

"Colt?"

"I asked you a question."

He hadn't asked her a question. He'd asked her to give away her flesh and blood. Their baby. She wanted to run, the very idea suddenly creating panic. How could she do this?

She gazed into his dark eyes, at the pain within. How could she not? Colt Raintree needed a family. A woman who loved him. A child. Melanie reached for his hand. She would tell him what he wanted to hear. Convince him to conceive a child with her.

His callused hand abraded hers. She squeezed it. He would fall in love with her before the baby was born, and later he would understand why she had kept her identity a secret. He would forgive her. After all, compassion had been what their past relationship was based on. How many times had he made her smile when she'd been on the verge of tears? And then there were the boosts of encouragement, the moments when he'd cupped her face and told her, "A smart girl like you can accomplish anything."

Melanie sighed. Although she had accomplished plenty over the years, she still hadn't fulfilled her biggest dream. Melanie Richards had yet to win Colt Raintree's heart. "I want to give you a child, Colt. I know what this means to you."

He withdrew his hand, then placed it in his lap, his posture stiff. "How can you want to do this for me? You don't even know me. There has to be more to it than that. Women have all sorts of reasons for becoming surrogates. But you haven't offered one logical explanation."

Melanie tilted her chin. She had a logical explanation. Loving him was reason enough to expect to share a child with him. And then there were the hardships in her life, the things she had overcome. The accident had made her stronger, more determined to go after what she wanted. Life was too short to waste.

"I told you I was a foster child. Of course, that impacted my life, made me who and what I am," she said. "I've learned to be comfortable and strong on my own. Yet, a piece of me wants to be part of a family, or at least know I contributed to one. It would give me a sense of peace to give someone a child. To know that I'd completed their family in some way. I could go on with my career, live my life and know it had purpose."

She saw him weakening. Her words had penetrated his heart, yet they were twisted. The explanation she had given was the very reason she longed to keep Colt's child and marry him.

"Would you think about the baby? Feel guilty about giving it away?"

She smiled softly. He looked as though he almost felt guilty for asking her to do it. "How could I, knowing it's your child? It would be well loved. And when I'd think about it, I'd envision it in your arms. Happy and smiling."

She could see him in her mind's eye, holding their baby, cuddling the tiny life against his broad chest. Only she imagined herself standing beside him, sharing the moment. Melanie's smile faded. The real possibility of having to give him that child made her ache. What if Colt didn't fall in love with her? She'd lose him and their baby.

"Do you want to see Meagan's room?" he asked. "I want you to know her in some way. If you have my baby, it would be her brother or sister."

She nodded silently and followed Colt down the hall. She'd been inside his house once before but only as far as the living room sofa.

The first time he had spoken to her was when she had fallen from one of his family's rental horses and sprained her ankle. Abandoned by her horse, Colt had spotted the disloyal beast galloping back to the stable and rode out looking for the horseless rider. He'd found her lying on a grassy slope, lifted her in his muscular arms, gently slung her over his mount, took her to his ranch and packed her ankle with ice. She had sat on the cowhide sofa, nervously chewing her fingernails, her heart melting while he wrapped her swollen ankle.

After that life-altering experience, she'd discovered someone other than Colt had suspected she was smitten. Someone who must have felt compelled to mention it.

Shorty Miller, the ornery old ranch hand who saddled the rental horses hadn't said beans to her until he'd learned about her mishap. When Melanie had returned to the stables the weekend following her injury, Shorty, a balding, beanpole of a man, sent a gruff compliment her way. "You stick with it, girlie," he'd said, adjusting her stirrup. "You've got a natural seat. Someday you'll be ridin' just fine, real prettylike."

Melanie had smiled proudly from atop the mount Shorty had chosen for her and scanned the grounds for Colt. "The boy ain't here," the old man had grumbled, his thick mustache twitching. "Took a group into the hills not more than twenty minutes ago."

Melanie had blushed from the top of her straw hat to the tips of her boots. "What boy?"

"Don't play me for a fool. The one you got yer eye on, girlie," had come the gravelly reply.

Week after week, Shorty had quietly pointed out Colt's whereabouts. "The boy's in the barn." "He just rode out." "He's team penning in the arena."

In the end, it had been Shorty who had informed her of Colt's impending nuptials. "The boy's gone and done it this time," the old man had said. "Got a girl in trouble, that one did. He'll be marrying her right quick."

Colt's husky voice jarred her back to the present. "Melanie, are you all right?"

They were standing in Meagan's room. *Got a girl in trouble, that one did.* Somehow, she didn't think Colt had ever thought of his daughter as trouble. "I'm fine."

She found herself surrounded in feminine delight. A pink canopy bed overflowed with stuffed animals and a large bay window was covered in eyelet and rose-tinted lace. White shelves displayed a porcelain doll collection, each dressed in hand-tailored finery. The wood toy box in the corner was ornately carved.

"I used to read to her every night," Colt said. "People think you should stop grieving after a few years. They don't understand that the loss of a child never goes away. It's always there, like a dull ache."

Melanie watched him. He picked up a stuffed lion from the bed and stroked its mane. "And they thought it was weird that I kept her room the way it was. But it wasn't as if I was trying to create a shrine. I thought that if I dismantled this room then I'd have nothing left of her."

He gazed around. "But you know, since I've decided to bring another child into my life, I'm actually ready to pack up my daughter's things. I thought this room would make a great nursery for the new baby. I'm sure Meagan would approve."

Melanie walked over to the dresser. A framed portrait displayed a younger, smiling Colt cuddling a dark-haired little girl. Her eyes were wide and brown, her skin a rich, glowing copper. "She was beautiful."

Colt replaced the fluffy lion. "Thank you."

Our child will be beautiful, too, Melanie thought, running her fingers along the edge of the frame. "I believe when babies are born, there's a guardian angel assigned to look after them. Meagan's probably been waiting for you to have another baby. I'm sure she's earned her wings by now."

Within a heartbeat, Colt was standing behind her, the faint, spicy scent of his cologne wafting to her nostrils. "You say nice things," he offered quietly. "I like you."

She turned and faced him. They were inches apart but she had to tilt her chin to view his expression. He towered over her by nearly a foot. Her Western boots didn't help much; he was also wearing a pair. "I like you, too."

He stepped back slowly, widening the space until they were standing a respectable distance apart. For an instant, adoration flickered in his fathomless gaze. It flashed by like a shooting star. She made a wish.

"Would you be interested in helping me redecorate this room?" he asked. "After all, you're the artist."

Had her wish just been granted? Was that his way of saying he wanted her for his surrogate? "I love furniture shopping. Antique stores are my favorite."

His dark eyes lit up. "Mine, too. I don't know about an old crib, though. Some of those early designs weren't too safe."

A surge of adrenaline rushed through her. "We can improvise. Mix new and old. I think you should keep the toy box, though. It would fit right in with what I have in mind."

Colt laughed. "You already have something in mind? You work fast, pretty lady."

Pretty lady. She liked that. "I'm good at what I do."

"Oh, yeah?" He crossed his arms over his massive chest and grinned. "Maybe you'd care to share some of those ideas floating around in your head."

"Okay." She pointed to the wall opposite the window. "The crib goes there. And here—" she turned and gestured "—would be the perfect spot for a rocking horse."

He studied her enthusiasm through amused eyes. "That's it?"

"No." She thrust a playful fist forward; it barely grazed a rock-hard shoulder. "We need to find a marvelous old cradle to keep the stuffed animals in. Something from the 1800s maybe. The nursery should reflect the Western motif of the house. Of course, we're going to have to add something colorful and animated, a paper border or some stenciled figures. Babies love bright colors."

Colt gazed intently at her. The half smile on his lips turned into a straight, serious line. "Melanie, we need to talk." He glanced over at his daughter's picture. "Let's go to the living room."

Moments later the door to Meagan's room was closed and Colt and Melanie were seated side by side on the cowhide sofa, the same one they had briefly shared thirteen years prior. The room was as she remembered it. Two brown leather recliners faced a stone hearth. An oak gun rack, timber wolf pelts and a bison head instilled the spirit of the west.

Colt's handsome features looked harsh, even in the dim light. The tiny lines around his eyes were almost white against his bronze skin, his lips still set in a tight frown. The shape of his lips fascinated her. The upper was perfectly formed and the full-ness of the lower created a natural, sensuous pout. The last time they had sat on the sofa together, she had studied that rakish pout. It had looked friendlier then.

Her stomach quivered. Had he decided she wasn't the right surrogate? Had her excitement over the nursery given her away? "What's the matter?" she asked, fearing the answer.

He pulled a hand through his unbound hair. "Maybe I jumped the gun about decorating the baby's room so soon. The kid hasn't even been conceived yet. And there are still a lot of issues that haven't been discussed—legal documents, financial and medical arrangements." He winced, as though his next words were forming a bitter taste in his mouth. "I hate to bring this up, but truthfully, it still bothers me that you're not what I ex-pected."

Her professional side took over, the one that marketed con-cepts, drawings and ideas. It was too late to become the surrogate he had envisioned, but it wasn't too late to promote the qualities she had. "How we imagine things is rarely how they really are. You want a woman who's willing to give up a child, but you think she should be the stereotype of a fifties TV mom. That's unrealistic, Colt."

Below the pout, a muscle ticked. "I know."

"What is it about me that concerns you?"

He kicked a booted foot onto the knotty-pine coffee table. "You're successful, talented and beautiful."

She sputtered a laugh. "Such terrible qualities. Your son or daughter might inherit them."

"It's not the kid I'm worried about," he admitted with his usual candor. "It's me. I had expected to feel a little more...clinical toward the woman I'm considering."

Melanie withheld a satisfied smile. Apparently Colt found himself attracted to her. "You're successful, talented and good-looking, too," she said, eyeing him appreciatively. "It's okay for us to admire each other. We're human beings. This shouldn't be 'clinical.' I don't want to be thought of as just a *hired womb*. From my understanding, the most successful surrogate relationships are the ones that stem from friendship."

Colt's features relaxed, frown lines fading. "Friends I can handle." His gaze dropped to the floor. "Did you bring a pair of sensible boots with you, California girl?"

She lifted her ostrich covered feet. "Sensible?"

"Plain old leather. Something to ride in."

"Are we riding?"

"Tomorrow at dawn. I supply the horses."

"Does that offer include scrambled eggs and coffee?"

"Sure." Colt smiled. "We'll talk babies over breakfast."

Melanie studied the delicious curve of his lip. "You've got yourself a deal, Montana man."

The following morning Colt smiled at the lady seasoning the hash browns. He liked her, this classy California girl, even though he had never been around her "type." Maybe she'd grown up in his hometown, but he envisioned her sunning on the beach, working out in an upscale gym and shopping in Beverly Hills. Who would have guessed she was surrogate-mother material?

She sprinkled bits of freshly-chopped garlic over the potatoes. Good thing they weren't going to kiss, he thought, surprising himself by the spontaneous notion. Melanie was the first woman in a long time he actually wanted to kiss.

Make love to.

Colt shook his head, trying to expel the unwelcome desire. Lovemaking and babies. The two, of course, were meant to go hand in hand. Just not in this case. If he made her pregnant it would be done in a doctor's office by way of a syringe. He did not want an emotional involvement in his life, and even though sex didn't always lead to one, an affair with his surrogate was asking for trouble. With a capital *T*.

"Where exactly in California do you live?" he asked.

She had already begun setting the table. From the moment she'd arrived, she'd rolled up her designer sleeves and pitched right in, chopping potatoes and squeezing oranges. Colt allowed his gaze to roam over her backside. Her jeans were a little too tight for proper ranch wear, but he didn't mind.

Melanie turned and smiled, silverware in hand. She had a genuine smile. A nice feature his child might inherit.

"Santa Monica. As close to the ocean as I could get."

He tried not to widen his eyes. Ostrich cowboy boots and the beach. "Isn't that expensive?"

"Not as expensive as Malibu. And I live in a condo, a leased one."

He cracked another egg into a mixing bowl, then tried to fish out a renegade shell that had settled with it. "But still…even a rental next to the ocean must cost a small fortune."

"It's worth it." She watched him chase the eggshell around with a tablespoon. "Colt, do you need some help?"

"Actually, yes, I do." He grinned. "I'm not too macho to admit when I need a woman." Immediately he bit back his grin, wishing he could bite back his words. "In the kitchen, I mean," he added, much too late.

Melanie handled his blunder like the true lady she was, ignoring it, much to his relief. "Here." She took the spoon and scooped out the shell on her first try. He stood nearby while she finished his original task. The eggs were cracked with one hand, shells discarded quickly.

Colt liked having her in such close proximity so he didn't move away. Instead he made a point of watching her scramble the eggs as though her culinary skills fascinated him. Her deft movements reminded him of his grandmother in the kitchen, of happier times and his favorite meals.

Colt took pleasure in having a woman cook for him. Of

course, not enough to welcome one back into his life, but what harm was there in allowing her to fix breakfast? "I'm great on an outdoor grill or over a campfire, but I never liked to fuss in the kitchen much."

Melanie poured the eggs into a pan, immediately stirring them with a rubber spatula. "Well then, we ought to get along just fine. I can never get the charcoal lit, and I don't know the first thing about campfires."

Ten minutes later they shared breakfast in the dining room, at the table his grandmother used to dust religiously with lemon oil. Colt noticed Melanie ate sparingly and avoided the bacon all together. He thought about teasing her about being a "cheap date," but decided it would probably be in bad taste. There was nothing cheap about their impending relationship.

Colt gobbled up the bacon she had rejected. "So, when are you going back to California?"

"I have to head back by the end of next week for a couple of business meetings. If and when I come back to Montana depends on—" a bright blue gaze met his "—what you decide."

Colt bit the inside of his lip, an irritating if not painful habit. Once he divulged the skeleton in his closet, would Melanie Richards want to bear his child?

"If *we* decide on this arrangement," he said, "I was wondering where you plan on living, because a long-distance pregnancy isn't what I had in mind. I want to be involved the way a father should be, attending doctor visits."

Melanie had a quick response. "The lease is almost up on my condo, so moving back to Montana isn't a problem. I can pretty much work from anywhere, as long as I meet my deadlines. And since the situation would be temporary, Gloria said I could stay with her." She sipped her juice. "But I'd rather get my own place. She already has eight kids underfoot. They don't need me and my art supplies taking up space."

He smiled. She always managed to say all the right things, put him at ease. "This house used to be a lodge. I've got an empty cabin out back. Maybe you could take up residence there."

"A cabin?" Her eyes sparkled. "That might be just what I need. I have to admit I miss Montana. The rat race in L.A. gets to me sometimes. And the rent has to be more reasonable than a beachfront condo, right?"

Colt realized they were both acting as though she were already his surrogate. "If you become my surrogate, there's no way I'd expect you to pay rent. I intend to cover your housing and medical expenses in addition to the fee we talked about." He couldn't resist a wink. "I'll even buy your groceries. You need to eat more, put some meat on those tiny bones of yours."

She laughed. "Oh, I think pregnancy might take care of that."

Colt finished his coffee. "How would you feel about me being present at the birth?"

A soft blush rose in her cheeks. "I don't know...I hadn't thought about— Were you there when Meagan was born?"

He nodded. "Most incredible experience of my life."

The pink stain on her cheeks remained. "Maybe we could start with those birthing classes and work up to the actual event."

Colt smirked. "Don't tell me you're modest. I thought California girls ran around in those itty-bitty bikinis."

She crossed her arms over her chest. "That's entirely different."

His body temperature rose a degree. Melanie in a skimpy bikini was a pleasant thought. "Why don't you talk to Gloria about the actual event? She must be a pro by now. And speaking from experience, women forget all about modesty when they're delivering a baby."

Melanie looked up from her unfinished meal. "Do you always say everything that's on your mind?"

"Pretty much."

But not always. He wouldn't dare say what was on his mind now. She was concerned about modesty? What about his part in the insemination?

Colt had already discussed the clinical details with the doctor. Fresh sperm versus frozen. Heck of a thing for a guy to have to contemplate. After weighing the facts, he'd opted fresh since usually twice as many inseminations were required with frozen.

He gazed at the beautiful woman seated across from him and couldn't help wishing another option was available. What? Penetration instead of insemination? He had no business entertaining that thought. None whatsoever.

Three

As she and Colt strode across the grounds to the barn, Melanie noticed it had been refurbished since the last time she had seen it. Everything was the same, yet different. The east side of the ranch still yielded a rodeo arena, the west, a chicken coop no longer clucking with life. There were almost as many horses as there had been, but a lot fewer steers.

Most of all, she was different. Inside and out. Gertrude Richards had been tucked away, and Melanie, confident California artist had emerged. Colt, too, it seemed had changed. True, his silky, black mane and heart-stopping wink were the same, but the wild teenage boy was gone. The brisk Montana winds had carried him away and brought back a man—mature, strong and proud, as rooted to the land as a tall ponderosa pine.

Colt went into the tack room while Melanie waited in the barn, amusing herself with a friendly mare. As she stroked the horse's blaze, it nodded in approval. In the next stall, a flashy, red dun gelding poked out its big, snorting nose and whinnied. "Just like a male," she said to the mare, "always looking for attention."

Colt's laughter sounded behind her. "Young Rocky there doesn't even know he's male. Now, I've got a champion stallion—Outlaw's Fancy…"

Melanie smiled. It figured Colt owned a stud named Outlaw. She motioned to the mare. "What's her name?"

He placed a bucket of grooming aids on the ground. "Sweet Cinnamon Surprise."

She eyed the gentle mare. The feminine name fit. "Sounds like a dessert I used to order at this trendy coffee bar on Melrose. I want to ride her."

Colt chuckled again. "Just like a woman to pick a horse for its pretty name."

Her chin tilted. "I do the same thing at the track. Sometimes I even win."

He looked amused by her admission. "Can you ride, California girl? I don't want Cinnamon taking advantage of you."

The chin protruded even further. "Of course I can ride. I was born in Montana, remember?" Besides riding on his ranch for nearly two years, she had also taken expensive lessons in California. Western pleasure and a little dressage. She wasn't the best dressage rider, but she looked good in the tall, black boots. "I can saddle a horse, too."

"Good." Colt reached for the halter and lead line hanging from a nail. "Put this on Cinnamon and hitch her up outside. I'll get a bridle and look for a saddle that will fit you." His gaze sparked appreciatively as it slid down her petite curves. "You sure are a little one."

"How does that saying go?" she asked, doing her best to seem innocent of his masculine stare. She didn't think he was aware of the hungry look in his eyes. "Something about small things…"

"*Good* things," he corrected, spinning on his heel, his husky voice fading as he departed. "Come…in…small…pack—"

"Like babies," Melanie whispered to Cinnamon as she buckled the nylon halter and led the mare into the summer sun. A bright blue sky, horses frolicking in lush green pastures, and a mountain backdrop greeted her. In the distance she could see some of Colt's ranch hands milling around. Behind the main house several rustic log cabins stood, one possibly waiting for her occupancy.

After securing the mare to a long, wooden hitching post, Melanie went back for the grooming supplies Colt had placed on the barn's dirt floor. Holding the curry in one hand and dandy in the other, Melanie brushed Cinnamon, then began picking out the sorrel's feet.

"Hey, Melanie."

She placed the mare's foot back on the ground and turned to the sound of Colt's voice. Someone else stood beside him. A tall, lanky man with a bushy, gray mustache. She recognized him immediately.

"This is Shorty," Colt said to her. "He's about the only family I've got left."

"The boy and me ain't related," the older man offered gruffly. "But I've been working this here ranch since before he was even born."

She didn't extend her hand. Both men carried saddles. "Nice to meet you. I'm Melanie."

Shorty balanced the saddle on his bony hip and tipped his dusty, tan hat. "Ma'am."

Colt slid the saddle in his arms over the hitching post rail and Shorty did likewise. She assumed the smaller one was hers. "Should I tack Cinnamon up?" she asked, hoping to avert Shorty's scrutinizing gaze by turning away. The old man's head was cocked in a birdlike pose.

"Sure, if you'd like," Colt answered. "Everything's there. The pad's underneath. I'll go get Rocky. He's still a little green on the trail. He could use the time out."

As Colt's long, denim-clad legs carried him back to the barn, Shorty stepped forward. "You look a tad familiar," he said.

"I grew up in the area. I live in California now."

He snorted. "You and the boy old friends?"

The boy. "No, we've just recently become acquainted." A truthful lie at best, since they had never really gotten to know each other in the past, at least not in the way she would have liked. There had been no romantic ties, at least not on Colt's end. But he would have been blind not to have suspected her amorous feelings. No, the last thing she needed was Shorty blowing her cover. If Colt found out who she was, he might think twice about using her as his surrogate.

Shorty smoothed his peppered mustache. He didn't look as old as he should. Maybe he hadn't been as ancient as she remembered. At seventeen anyone over forty seemed like a fossil.

He wagged a long, slightly crooked finger. "I'm sure I've met you somewhere."

Melanie reached for the bridle slung over the saddle horn, trying to appear too busy to chat. "Mountain Bluff is a small town."

"It will come to me," Shorty mumbled as he strode away. "I never forget a face."

"You've been awful quiet." Colt reined his gelding to a stop and glanced over at Melanie. "Is something bothering you?"

Cinnamon halted without being asked. "No, I've just been taking in the scenery." And worrying sick over Shorty's last words. Should she tell Colt who she was? Would it matter to him?

Of course it would, she told herself, once again.

"Do you want to stretch your legs a bit?" he asked.

"Okay."

How accurate could Shorty's memory be? she wondered as they dismounted. The man had worked on a recreational ranch for over thirty years. Most likely he had met hundreds of people. He couldn't possibly remember them all and especially not a girl whose features had been altered.

Melanie watched Colt hobble the horses, and decided it was time to relax and enjoy the land. They had been riding for hours and in truth she hadn't taken in the scenery at all. In doing so now, a wave of homesickness washed over her.

Patches of wildflowers colored the terrain, their tiny, bright heads swaying in a gentle breeze. Trees stood tall and green, gnarled roots clawing the rich soil, tiny animals nesting within.

Mountains peaked to an enormous summer sky filled with clouds so downy and white, she imagined tiny blonde cherubs peering over the floating cushions, bows taut, amorous arrows poised for flight. This, she thought, was definitely the place to fall in love. Just a breath away, a small stream moistened the floral-scented air, bubbling and polishing stones as it moved, the clear water cool and inviting. Serenity. Pure and simple.

"I forgot how beautiful Montana is," Melanie said, kneeling beside the stream.

"This is my favorite spot." Colt moved toward her with long-legged grace, the ends of his shoulder-length hair fluttering like sleek, black wings. He placed a water flask on the ground between them and followed it down. "I feel content here."

"I can see why." She picked up a pinecone and studied it. "I used to collect these all year, then paint them at Christmas-time. I still make all my own ornaments." Suddenly the need to move back to Montana grew fierce. "After all these years, waking up at the beach on Christmas morning still feels strange. That's when I miss snow the most."

He drew his legs up and leaned his elbows against his knees. A Stetson as dark as his eyes rested on his head, a blue denim shirt covered the broad expanse of his chest. Melanie glanced down at her own shirt; it was denim too, only it yielded a de-signer's label. Colt's probably came from the Western Empo-rium in town. He was a wealthy man but a simple one. She had heard his grandfather had made some sound investments, leaving Colt with quite a nest egg.

He looked over at her. "Do you ever visit your foster family during the holidays?"

Melanie cupped the pinecone and met his curious gaze. "No. They moved away years ago. Besides, I only lived there for a couple years, during high school. I'd been shuffled around a lot. Mostly city homes. I didn't really grow up in Mountain Bluff, but I fell in love with it." *Because you were here.* "And I was lucky enough to live next door to Gloria. Her family treated me like one of their own. I tell people this is my hometown because Gloria's still here." *And so are you.*

"I guess that explains why we never met. I pretty much know everyone who grew up around here or have at least heard of them, but if you only lived here for a few years..." He grinned. "You really are a city girl, aren't you?"

"I suppose I am."

"You mentioned Saint Theresa's the other night. I used to know some girls who went there." Colt paused, then shrugged. "But I can't recall their names. It's been a while."

She remembered a few girls from her high school had briefly dated some of Colt's buddies. She had always thought that they had spread her despised nickname around Colt's elite circle.

"You're such a mystery," he said, leaning forward to skim his hand across the water. "I'm an open book...but you—"

"Then come to California with me," Melanie blurted.

Beneath the Stetson, his features startled. "You're kidding, right?"

"Not at all." She assumed her "sales pitch" posture, squaring her shoulders and tilting her chin confidently. She didn't want to be so much of a mystery that it hindered his final decision. Colt seemed suspicious by nature, or had acquired the habit after his wife had kidnapped their daughter. Apparently trust didn't come easily. That thought saddened her. Colt had been so trusting in the past, free spirited with a sense of humor. She intended to bring that part of him back.

"I'm assuming that if you were considering a surrogate who lived in Montana, you'd visit her home, see how she lived, meet her husband and kids. Of course, with me, there's no husband, no kids and no home to visit, at least not in Montana. But if you come back to California with me, you could see for yourself who I really am. Clear up the mystery and ease your conscience."

A majestic hawk circling overhead made a breathtaking sight but Colt didn't appear to notice. He continued swishing the water as though deep in thought. Melanie fixed her gaze on the shadow of his bronzed hand beneath the surface of the stream. The water swirled around his fingers in clear, blue circles.

"We can't drag this decision on forever," she said, continuing her rationale. "Figure it this way—if we go to California together and you feel comfortable about my background, then I can tie up my loose ends there and come back here for the insemination."

Colt lifted his gaze, removed his wet hand and dragged it

across his jaw. "There's something about me I think you ought
to know. Something I should have told you before now."

She flashed a teasing smile. She knew all she needed to know.
In her eyes this man was perfect. "I thought you were an open
book—"

"I'm a recovering alcoholic."

Colt's startling admission rammed her like a fist, jolting her
mind with disturbing images of her youth. They filled her with
despair: the pungent smell of cheap liquor permeating a dingy
apartment, stale bread for lunch, nothing for dinner, unkind men
frequenting her mother's rumpled bed. She remembered ironing
her own tattered clothes and getting herself off to school while
the woman who had given her life lay in a drunken stupor. The
day the authorities had placed her in foster care, her mother had
solemnly promised to "do better." She never had. Melanie had
remained in the system until her eighteenth birthday.

"You drink?"

He steadied his gaze, spearing her with his guilt. "Used to.
Partied a lot when I was a kid, got drunk for the hell of it, like
teenagers do. It didn't appear to be a problem, though, because
I grew out of that phase when Meagan came along." His fingernails scraped the dirt, imbedding the ground with catlike
scratches. "But after she died... I hit the bottle pretty bad. The
year she was missing I lived on hope...after I buried her, there
was nothing left... nothing mattered. I've been sober, going on
five years now, but it's been a rough road, and I'm not sure I
could have made it without Shorty. He never gave up on me."

Melanie couldn't think of anything to say. Because of her
mother, alcoholics had always been intolerable in her mind. Yet
this was Colt, the man who had helped heal her wounded teenage heart. If someone as beautiful as him had defended her, she
used to tell herself, then she must be special, worth much more
than her biological mother had thought her to be.

Colt's humble voice interrupted the silence. "I hope this
doesn't affect your decision. Because I want you to know, no
matter what hardship comes my way, I won't choose alcohol as
a remedy. I was a disgrace to my daughter's memory, as well

as to myself. I'd never consider bringing another child into my life if I had the slightest doubt about my sobriety.''

Melanie looked at the man questioning her gaze and did something she had hoped never to do in his presence. Burst into tears.

For a long uncomfortable moment, Colt just stared, uncertain of what to do. Although his first instinct was to draw her into his arms, he refrained. If he touched her and she shattered, broke into a million vulnerable little pieces right there in his arms, he'd be tempted to kiss the hurt away. To place his lips on every salty drop and taste her sadness. He recognized tears that ached, he'd shed enough of them.

"Do you want to talk about it?"

"No...yes...I don't know..." She covered her face with trembling hands.

He moved closer, knelt down beside her and cursed his knotting stomach. He tamed horses. This sweet little creature was a woman. "I'm sorry if I said something to upset you."

She dropped her hands. The dark smudges of mascara around her eyes made her look like a blue-eyed raccoon. Adorable, yet destructive to a man's conscience—the kind of trophy he'd feel guilty about later.

"I wish she'd have cared enough to stay sober," Melanie muttered bitterly.

"She?"

The dam looked like it might break again. Another flood of tears gathered in her eyes. "My mom."

Colt swallowed. "Your mom was an alcoholic?"

She nodded. "My childhood wasn't easy."

"I'm sorry," he said. "You deserved better."

"Yes, I did." She blinked her tears back. "But it took a long time for me to believe that. I waited for my mom to change, to take me back home and live a normal life." Her distraught gaze avoided his as her hand nervously picked at the pinecone, chipping pieces off. "But that never happened."

"Is your mom still alive?"

She shrugged. "I don't know. I've lost touch with her. Is yours?"

"No." Colt couldn't contain the sadness in his tone. "My mom died of cancer when I was still a boy."

She looked up and dropped the broken pinecone sending it into the stream. "I'm sorry."

Colt removed the bandana around his neck, dipped a corner of it into the stream and gently cleaned Melanie's mascara-stained cheeks. The stricken blue gaze belonged to the neglected daughter of an alcoholic, the chic California girl hidden somewhere deep within. For one brief moment his lonely heart tagged after both.

"Life is hard sometimes," he said.

"Yes, it is," she whispered.

When they both fell silent, the beauty around them intensified: the morning sun teasing the jagged rocks, gold-tipped leaves rustling through the trees, the rush of cool water, his admiring gaze, her smooth skin.

Colt tucked her hair behind her ear and handed her the red cloth. She dabbed her runny nose with the dry portion. "I feel better now," she said. "Thank you."

"Good." He smiled and reached for her hair again. The fire-lit strands slipped through his fingers like ribbons of silk. When she leaned toward his caressing hand, he realized how intimate their gestures were. "Are you still willing to be my surrogate?"

"Yes." Her breathless voice sent a surge of sensual heat coursing through his veins.

Colt shuddered. He wouldn't permit this to happen. He wouldn't confuse his need for a child with desire for the woman willing to carry it. That's what was happening, he told himself. He was vulnerable and so was she. Their physical compulsion to produce a baby was creating false intimacy. His urge to taste her citrus-scented skin and run his hands through her thick, autumn hair would go away once his seed was planted. Artificially, of course.

Colt transferred his hand from her hair to the water flask and took a cold, desire-dousing drink. As casually as he could muster, he uncoiled his long body and rose to his feet. "I think California is a good idea. And not because you need to be on trial. We're both about sure as we're going to get, so we may as well start on the legal and medical side of this. And you'll probably need some help getting packed.''

Her smudgy eyes brightened, but he kept his expression tight and professional. ''Before we leave for Los Angeles, we'll see my attorney and get the contract drawn up so you can consult your own lawyer back home and have him look it over.''

''Her,'' Melanie interjected.

''What?''

''My attorney is a woman.''

''Fine. You also need to make an appointment with Dr. Miller for a checkup, and of course, to discuss the best method of determining ovulation.'' He caught her amused smirk and prayed to God he wouldn't stutter like a flustered schoolboy. ''I don't want to waste any time, I want you ready for the procedure when we return.''

He cursed his traitorous body for what it wanted and continued in an unemotional tone. ''I'll hire a moving van and pay the storage fee for the things you don't bring. Maybe you should consider subleasing your condo so you don't lose it. I imagine a beachfront rental is hard to come by.''

''What altered your decision?'' she asked, viewing his towering height from the ground. ''I expected you to ponder over this for weeks.''

He resisted the nervous urge to pace. Regardless of the wide-open space, he felt like a caged tiger, trapped within his own distorted desire. ''I've been thinking about this for years and meeting with potential surrogates for the past eight months—''

''You have?'' She stood up and brushed off her behind.

''Yeah. And I've met with a lot of women. No one seemed right.'' Not the fifties TV moms or the desperate ones with financial needs. He couldn't see his unborn child in their eyes. With Melanie he could.

''What makes me right?''

Great Scott. Just like a woman to question a man to death, force him to spill his guts. ''Maybe the idea that you're single is growing on me. The fewer people involved the better. And the fact that you're a career woman is a plus, too. I hadn't thought so at first but with you being so into your profession, I won't have to worry about your maternal instincts backfiring on me. My biggest concern is my surrogate deciding she wants the baby, but with you, I figure that won't happen.''

''Oh.'' She glanced down at her jeans and began dusting off her knees.

Was his explanation so cold that she couldn't meet his gaze? Damn it. He wasn't about to tell her he wanted his child to inherit her smile.

''I like you, Melanie. That means something, too. I feel as though we've known each other for a while. As you said, being friends is important. We don't want to get on each other's nerves for the next nine months.''

She offered a smile that went straight to his groin. Thank God pregnant women didn't really glow. His wife had whined and complained the entire time, making the gestation pretty darn unappealing. How attractive could Melanie possibly be in that state?

Colt's jaw twitched. This California girl was going to bear him a child, but damn if he would allow her to get under his skin. This friendship would be short-lived. Fatherhood was the only emotional attachment Colt Raintree wanted, or needed. Once his son or daughter was born, Melanie Richards would be out of his life. For good.

Four

LAX had annoyed him. Actually, it more than annoyed him. The confusion of the fast-paced airport had made him feel like a big, dumb, country boy. Colt Raintree, Montana born and bred, was out of his element.

Rather than breathing crisp mountain air, he was choking down smog and riding shotgun in a red convertible piloted by an auburn-haired beauty who made Mario Andretti seem like a slowpoke.

"How about some music?" Melanie turned the knob on the stereo and started punching buttons.

She settled on a country station, for his benefit, he assumed. Willie Nelson's nasal twang should have been a balm, but it only reminded Colt of how far from home he was. The unfamiliar roar of traffic offended the simple cowboy tune.

Melanie glanced over her shoulder, switched lanes and questioned his pouting profile. "Colt, what's wrong?"

He answered as honestly as he could. "I never cared much for cities."

Melanie slid her right hand from the steering wheel and placed it on top of his, which rested on the center console. "You'll like the beach," she promised with a quick, reassuring squeeze. "We're almost there."

She was right. The moment they exited the freeway and the sea breeze tousled his hair, he appreciated the freedom the rag top provided. When the Pacific Ocean came into view, a sense of well-being entered his soul. It looked as big as the Montana sky and just as blue.

Saltwater, fresh-grilled seafood, hot dogs and lemonade permeated the air. They passed a pier that looked like a street fair— a menagerie of blinking lights, twirling carnival rides and trendy teenagers, their colorful T-shirts, baggy shorts and bleached blonde hair whipping in the wind.

The sidewalks were lined with people, but they were different from the airport crowd. They moved at a pace his eyes could follow, dressed in sandals, suntan lotion and little else. Maybe it was the warrior in him, but the half-naked, bronzed bodies made him want to shed his own clothes, feel the sand between his toes, dive into the surf, let the sun beat down on his back.

He grinned at Melanie. Her unique style fit right in. "Interesting town."

"I knew you'd like it." She continued down the busy coast highway, turned onto a narrow street and then another, until she parked in the driveway of an attractive white building.

Her condominium faced the ocean. A wood staircase led to the front door, elevating the modern structure. Just like her denim and silk wardrobe, the eclectic style reflected the woman who lived there. A marble coffee table, gilt-framed mirrors and contemporary artwork were surrounded by seashells and scented candles. White leather sofas highlighted an exquisite fireplace, meticulously carved of polished stone.

Colt placed their luggage on the living room floor and peered out the French doors. A redwood deck lush with potted plants, rattan furnishings and a whirlpool tub graced his eyes. Seaside elegance at its finest.

"Your house is really nice." He had planned on booking a hotel room, but Melanie had extended her California hospitality, persuading him to stay with her. Their platonic relationship was off to an awkward start. Her condo seemed like a romantic get-away, a honeymoon suite.

"Thanks." She glanced down at the suitcases. "I'll show you to your room. It has a private bath, so if you want to freshen up…"

Freshen up? As in strip down and shower? Unconsciously he took a step back. "I think I should get a hotel room."

She sank into one of the leather sofas and sighed. "Why?"

Because if I shower in your tub or sleep in one of your beds, I'll want you there beside me. "Your neighbors might talk."

Melanie looked as though he'd just said something incredibly stupid. "This is L.A., Colt."

When she crossed her legs, her ruffled miniskirt exposed just enough thigh to constrict his throat. He'd been trying to avoid the outline of her curvaceous little figure all day. On the plane ride, she had fallen asleep against his shoulder, her scant Hawaiian print blouse gaping open for a private peep show. Pink satin, a hint of lace and not one visible tan line. He'd never been so aroused.

"So?"

"So, people don't care what their neighbors do."

"Oh, yeah?" He trapped her gaze. "Would they talk if they knew you were going to be a surrogate?"

She held his dark stare. "Probably, but that's a little more controversial than having a man stay over."

"Really?" In his hometown, people still talked about who slept at whose house. Her casual attitude piquing him, he spouted off like an envious suitor. "And just how many men have stayed here?"

Her voice vibrated. "What exactly are you accusing me of?"

Colt only stared. She looked mortally wounded and, God help him, way too vulnerable. He gazed into Melanie's eyes and shook off a chill. Suddenly she looked like someone from his past—a sweet, innocent girl who had touched his reckless, teen-age heart.

The name came to him in an instant, hovering like a ghost. Gertrude. Little Gertrude. He glanced at Melanie's hands, at the slender line of her fingers, the long, perfectly manicured nails.

Gertrude used to chew her nails, gaze up at him with those wide blue eyes and nibble her chipped, brittle fingernails.

Colt sat on the edge of his suitcase and raked his hands through his hair, pushing away Gertrude's fragile image. "I'm not accusing you of anything. I'm sorry. I had no right to say that." What was wrong with him? He'd never felt possessive of a woman before. "I guess I've been thinking about how much gossip you and I are going to stir up back home."

"There's no way to avoid that." Melanie twisted a tassel on one of the decorative pillows. "Our situation is unusual."

He rocked the suitcase and tried not to stammer. "Sure, but…we could at least try to keep a low profile. Not dating other people while we're expecting might keep some of the tongues from wagging."

Colt blew an anxious breath and waited for her response. He couldn't stand the thought of Melanie being with another man while she carried his child, not even something as innocent as dinner or a movie.

Her near-timid smile warmed his heart. "Can we put that in the contract?" she asked. "Because you're the one who will still be trim and attractive. I doubt anyone's going to want to date me four or five months from now."

"I'll take you out so you don't get lonely," he said, telling himself it would be for the sake of the baby. "And I promise not to get involved with anyone if you don't." A married surrogate was one thing, but making a single woman pregnant and dating another seemed disrespectful. "A jealous lover could create stress and even more gossip," he said, trying to justify his odd request. "We don't need either."

When she promptly agreed and extended her hand, he clasped it in his. As they shook on the verbal agreement, Colt realized how unusual their situation was.

"And I am going to rent a hotel room while I'm here," he reiterated, breaking contact. Her fingertips were too soft, the feminine touch warm and inviting. "Regardless of what you say, people talk. I've tarnished enough reputations in the past. I don't need yours on my conscience, too."

The following evening Melanie convinced Colt to accompany her to the mall. They'd spent the morning apart and the afternoon together. She'd attended a business meeting while he explored the beach. By noon, they'd met for lunch and began packing immediately thereafter. He'd worked in the kitchen, she'd been in her bedroom. When she'd tackled the grueling task of organizing her closet and choosing a suitable Montana wardrobe, she'd decided shopping for fashionable maternity clothes was definitely in order.

Melanie scanned the blouse rack and peered up at Colt. Like most men in a woman's dress shop, he looked bored.

She held up a hideous shocking-pink number. "What do you think?"

He shrugged. "What am I supposed to say? I don't know anything about women's clothes. Besides, isn't it a little early for this?" He eyed the enormous blouse, then glanced around, apparently for eavesdroppers. "We haven't…you're not even…well, you know."

"I will be," Melanie proclaimed, her chin tilting. Per doctor's orders she'd been charting her temperature religiously. "And when I'm big enough for maternity fashions, I'll be knee-deep in snow and hours away from a decent mall. Mountain Bluff isn't exactly the shopping capital of the world."

"All right." He tossed his hands in the air. "Go ahead and pick out some fancy duds, but when we're back in Montana, I guarantee you'll be complaining that there's noplace to wear them."

"Oh, yeah?" She wagged a finger. "Well you, Mr. Raintree, promised to take me out."

A dark brow arched toward the hot-pink top. "Not in that."

Melanie crammed the blouse back onto the rack and grinned. "They have a chair over there." She pointed to a corner where she assumed other expectant fathers had waited. "I'll let you know when I'm ready."

He glanced back at the chair. "For what?"

Apparently Colt had never shopped with a woman before. "To model the clothes."

"Oh."

As he made his way to the corner, a middle-aged sales clerk flashed him an approving smile and offered assistance to Melanie. "Is there something special you're looking for?"

"Everything." She began counting months off on her fingers. If she conceived right away, she would probably start showing in November, maybe even October. "I'll need items for winter and spring."

The bubbled-haired blonde, who introduced herself as Penny, began escorting Melanie through the fashionable maternity boutique. They gathered several styles of leggings in an array of colors, long- and short-sleeved blouses, casual dresses for daily wear, black velvet for the holiday season.

Before the blonde secured the dressing room, she handed Melanie a pillow-type attachment. "It ties on," she said, when Melanie glanced at it curiously. "To give you a tummy."

She spent the next twenty minutes trying on fashions and sending Penny for size and color changes. The pillow-tummy was a shock. She giggled at first, then touched it unbelievably. If her own flesh was going to protrude this far, then it was time to show Colt how she was going to look.

Melanie patted the pillow, then slipped on a stylish white dress and fluffed her hair. "Here goes," she whispered, exiting the dressing room.

He was sitting in the chair where she left him, paging through a magazine the sales clerk must have offered, one tennis shoe tapping. She stood in front of the three-way mirror beside him.

"Colt?"

He looked up, slid the magazine under the chair, rose to his full height and stood behind her, gazing at her reflection. She followed the line of his eyes down her dress. The soft cotton material gathered beneath her breasts, flowed over her exaggerated tummy, then swirled around her ankles where a border of lilac ribbon added a touch of spring.

"It's a pillow they give you," she explained as his gaze rested on the fullness of her figure, "so you know how the clothes will fit later."

He moved closer, his pleased reflection behind her in the mirror. When he dipped his head, his warm breath tickled her nape.

"You look beautiful," he whispered, both hands instinctively coming forward.

She watched him, wishing she could feel his hands as they slid around a tummy that wasn't really hers. Is this how it will be? she wondered, leaning back against his tall frame, her knees weakening. *Will he caress the baby when it's cradled inside me?*

"Melanie?" Colt nuzzled her neck, his hands still wrapped around her waist. "Promise me something."

An erotic shiver tiptoed up her spine. They looked good together, their cheekbones high, their hair shiny and straight. Even the difference in their eyes seemed right. Hers shone like bright blue stars, and his were as dark and exotic as a midnight sky.

"Promise you'll stick by me, even if it takes a while to conceive." He rested his chin on her shoulder and gazed at her through the mirror. Melanie wondered if he was comparing reflections, creating their child's features in his mind. "I want it to be you."

"I promise," she answered. She'd stick by him forever if he'd let her. "I want it to be me, too."

The world stilled. They stood in a warm embrace, his hands worshipping the pillow beneath her dress as though it really were his child. Melanie melted against the rush of emotion washing through her. Colt's lips were against her neck, his spicy scent mingling with hers, his arms strong and protective. Her heartbeat doubled and his breath caught before the sales clerk's chipper voice broke the tender spell.

"You two must be newlyweds," she teased, darting by with a handful of garments for another customer, not bothering to glance back for a reaction.

Silence ricocheted. Colt's gaze found Melanie's in the mirror, and she expected him to smile, or tease her about the blush rising to her cheeks. He didn't. Instead, he flinched and pulled away. His shoulders jerked and his hands grew stiff as his handsome features turned to stone.

Melanie's body chilled.

"I guess we'll have to get used to comments like that," he said, sounding once again like her business partner. "But we shouldn't encourage it. I apologize for putting you in that position.''

"Of course," she responded, fighting back a choked scream, hurt and angry that he could switch gears so easily. There was no warmth in his apology, no compassion, a twitching jaw the only telltale sign of emotion.

"I'll go change." Melanie tore off quickly, locked the dressing room door and trembled, willing herself not to cry. Emerging sometime later, she strode over to the front counter and placed her purchases down, assuming the role as the unaffected surrogate. Colt stood by dispassionately, handing over a credit card when the balance was totaled. Melanie decided not to interfere or argue over payment in front of Penny, who, judging by her sympathetic behavior, must have thought the newlyweds had a tiff. Uncomfortable vibrations and awkward glances were far too apparent.

"Are you angry with me?"

It took Colt several days to acquire the courage to ask her that. They'd been packing nonstop, barely speaking to each other.

"No." She tore the package-sealing tape with her teeth, pressed it onto a box and snapped a fingernail in the process. Uttering a frustrated curse, she met his gaze. "I'm just exhausted."

She was upset. He could see it in her eyes, and he knew it was because of his behavior at the mall the other night. Only he wasn't sure if it was due to the fact that he'd touched her with such familiarity or had ended it so abruptly. Either way, it was something he shouldn't have done. He was confusing her, preying on her emotions with false intimacy.

Colt bit the inside of his lip. It had been false. Hadn't it?

He glanced at her broken fingernail. Once again he was reminded of the other blue-eyed girl, the one from his past. Little Gertrude. He shook away the disturbing image. Why did Melanie have to remind him of Gertrude? Of her gentle, doelike qualities?

"I'm sorry," he said.

"For what?" She whipped around his shoulder to examine the glass figurines he was packing. "Did you break something?"

"No...I'm just sorry for..." *Holding you? Enjoying it? Wishing I could do it again?* "Being so grumpy."

"That's okay." Melanie frowned at her fingernail. She looked young and sweet, her hair braided, her sundress sprinkled with printed flowers. "I know you're exhausted, too," she said, examining the damaged appendage. "I told you Tiffany was coming over, right?"

"Who?"

"Tiffany. The lady I'm designing the logo for."

He gave her a blank stare.

"She's opening the vintage clothing store. I told you about it."

"Oh, yeah. The Bandit." A combination of early Western wear and goofy seventies garb. The Lone Ranger meets the Brady Bunch. It sounded ridiculous to him. "She's the wacky one, right?"

"Eccentric," she corrected, as though it didn't mean the same thing. "Tiffany's bringing over some composites for me to look at. We need to decide on a model to use for the logo design. She wants a cowboy type, you know, rugged and handsome. Only we're going to stylize his look. Of course, we'll put him in a cowboy hat with a black mask around his eyes for the bandit effect, but to tie in the sixties and seventies, I'm going to do some psychedelic artwork on his chest."

"You're going to paint some guy's body?"

Melanie beamed. "Isn't it a great idea? Afterward, I'll use the model's photograph for a watercolor."

Colt furrowed his brow. "If the finished product is going to be a painting, then why are you going to put artwork on the model's body? Can't you add that in later?"

"Tiffany wanted me to do it this way. She wants the body art to look like it's part of his skin. The photograph will show us if the design has the desired effect."

He tapped on the boxtop. "Maybe I should go back to the hotel while you and Tiffany have your meeting." He didn't want to be present while two women ogled men's photographs, and he sure as hell didn't want to see a picture of the guy Melanie was going to body paint.

"Please stay," she implored. "Tiffany's as much a friend as a client. I want you to meet her."

Colt gazed around the dining room. It was nearly packed, the china cabinet shelves empty. "Did you tell her about us…about our arrangement?"

"No. I told her I was going back to Montana to stay with a friend, that I needed a change of scenery."

Great. Tiffany would probably take one look at him and think he was Melanie's lover. Since when would a woman travel half-way across the United States to stay with a man who's just a friend. "If you don't mind, I'll just keep packing while she's here."

"That's fine. I'll order us something to eat. She'll be here soon."

Melanie's friend arrived right after the pizza. Attired in a Western, rhinestone get-up Dolly Parton would envy, Tiffany lived up to her eccentric label. Tall, blond, and oddly attractive, her age hard to define, Colt suspected a face lift or two. Melanie had described her as "alimony rich," the vintage clothing store her latest form of amusement.

The women hugged and exchanged Hollywood kisses, their lips brushing by each other's cheeks, connecting with nothing but air. The brown-and-white-spotted dog Tiffany brought with her seemed genuine enough; it wagged its tail and jumped straight into Melanie's arms.

"JR, you little devil, how are you?" she cooed, nuzzling the little guy's face.

Colt almost expected the dog to respond. JR was an animated little critter with big expressive eyes and floppy ears.

"Well." Tiffany's gaze swept appreciatively over Colt. "You must be the Montana cowboy."

He extended his hand. "Colt Raintree."

"Nice name." She shook his hand, smoothed her silver-blond hair and winked at Melanie.

Yep, she thought they were lovers. "If you ladies will excuse me, I'm going to finish packing."

Unfortunately the only room left was the one Melanie and Tiffany would be occupying. Colt grabbed some pizza, opened a soda and sat down in front of the entertainment center to pack Melanie's CD collection. JR padded after him. He scratched the dog's head. It sat up and begged.

The women shared one of the leather sofas, nibbled on pineapple and pepperoni pizza and began paging through the photographs Tiffany had brought. Thirty minutes later, the "maybe" pile had just one picture, a model who freelanced as an exotic dancer.

"What about *him?*" Tiffany asked, lowering her voice.

"He is handsome," Melanie responded in the same quiet tone.

"He's perfect and you know it. Dark hair, dangerous eyes, a great body. And he's the genuine article. A real-live Montana rancher."

"He would look great in a black mask." Both women giggled. "And even better in body paint."

Okay, so they found their cowboy. A Montana man, no less. A ranch hand turned model. What a sissy. Colt resisted the urge to turn around and examine the guy's picture. Melanie sounded a little too impressed.

A real-live Montana rancher.

Colt spun around to find Melanie and Tiffany sizing him up like a side of beef.

"No way!" he shouted.

Tiffany framed him with her hands. "Oh, he's perfect."

Panic set in. "No…no, I'm not. I take a terrible picture…my eyes—" he crossed them "—are too close together…see?" When that failed, he pointed to his jaw. "And look at this scar—"

His imperfections were ignored. "Instead of a cloth mask, I'll paint it on," Melanie said. "Like a warrior."

The other woman gasped dramatically. "I love it!"

Melanie strode over to him. "You should see his chest. What a canvas. Not one speck of hair."

She began unbuttoning his shirt.

"I'm not posing for any pictures," he hissed. "And you're not—" she continued releasing buttons "—painting my body."

"Yes, I am." While pushing his shirt open, Melanie hummed a quiet tune that sounded remarkably like a lullaby. "You owe me," she whispered.

Was she bargaining for the baby? "Why, you little imp." When her fingertips grazed his nipples, he swallowed a groan. "This is blackmail."

She stood on the tips of her toes and pressed her mouth against his ear. "What's the matter, Montana man? Are you modest?"

"You don't play fair, California girl," he whispered back, catching her hands with his wrists. If she teased his nipples again, he'd fall at her feet and beg for more. "I'd never be able to show my face in town."

"We'll keep it a secret." She smiled playfully and freed her hands. "No one will ever know the painting was you."

From across the room, Tiffany watched them through amused eyes. "Now, Melanie, if Colt's not interested in the job…" She picked up the stripper's photograph. "I'm sure this attractive young man would be thrilled.…"

An image of Melanie running her hands over the dancer's body clouded Colt's judgment. "I'll do it," he growled, tugging his shirt closed. "But nobody, and I mean *nobody* better find out about this."

Five

After escorting Tiffany to her car, Melanie returned to the house to see Cold standing on the balcony gazing out at the ocean. She watched him, wondering how he would react if she tried to seduce him, run her hands up and down his broad back, press her body tightly against his.

If Melanie hadn't been aching to touch him so badly, she would have laughed. Seduce a man? Her? Geeky Gertie?

She was still a virgin.

Because of her mother's promiscuity, Melanie didn't believe in casual sex. She'd seen firsthand how easily a woman could cheapen herself with meaningless affairs. As a result, she had promised to respect herself—to remain a virgin until the right man came along. The man she loved. And from the first moment she'd seen Colt, she knew he was the one.

Of course, Colt had married someone else and she'd gone on without him. But even so, she'd remain true to herself—to her morality. For years she had strived to make herself beautiful, then rejected almost every man who came her way. The fact that men wanted her simply because of her looks bothered her.

She knew deep down that if any of those men had known her before her physical transformation, they wouldn't have given her the time of day.

In a sense, being in love with Colt had helped keep her virginity intact. Sure, she had dated other men, but hadn't fallen in love with any of them. And for her, sex without love was an impossibility. Besides, Colt was the one man who had treated her kindly before she was pretty. His compassion had been genuine. And now, even though he didn't recognize her, Melanie knew she was the same person, the same girl he had winked and smiled at, the same girl he used to call "cute and sweet." She couldn't help but love Colt Raintree.

When Colt turned around, her heart stopped. The man was beautiful, dangerous and kind, sexy, cautious, moody. The wind had tousled his hair and the front of his shirt was still unbuttoned, exposing smooth, muscular skin as dark and rich as a cup of cinnamon cappuccino sweetened with just a dash of cream.

Thoughts of seduction returned. God, if she only knew how. She moved forward, suddenly feeling shy. "Hi."

He smiled, and when he did, his entire face transformed. The sun-baked, masculine lines faded and he managed to look boyish once again. Not quite a warrior. "I was wondering if you had a sleeping bag I could borrow?"

"Sure, I have a couple, but I think they're packed. Why do you need one?"

He smoothed his windblown hair. She was half tempted to mess it up again, push her hands through it.

"I've been going a little stir-crazy in the hotel. I like wide-open spaces. I need to sleep outdoors once in a while." He glanced over his shoulder. "The beach is just too beautiful to resist."

Pleased that he shared her love of the ocean, she cursed her next words. "I don't think it's allowed, Colt."

He frowned and glanced back at the water again. "What do you mean? Like it's against the law or something?"

"Sort of, I think. I know there are beaches in California with designated camping areas, but none close by. I'm not sure what the law is around here." She'd never had cause to find out.

Sleeping on the beach at night had never occurred to her. "After a certain hour it might be considered vagrancy or loitering."

"That's too bad," Colt said with a dastardly grin, "because I'm sleeping there anyway. If I get busted, you'll just have to bail me out of jail."

"What if I get busted, too?" she asked in a subtle attempt to invite herself on his sleepover. Miles of sand, the sea at midnight and Colt Raintree. What a fantasy.

"Are you saying you want to sleep with me?" He countered her question, then flinched when he caught his own blunder. "Damn." The devilish grin faded. "I didn't mean that the way it sounded."

I wish you had. She wanted to sleep with him. Beneath him. Naked as the day she was born.

As Melanie met his smoky gaze, her cheeks heated, her own immodest thoughts making her blush. Thank goodness the balcony was dimly lit. "Camping on the beach sounds like an adventure I wouldn't want to miss."

When Colt's expression turned dark and altogether brooding, she ignored her flushed cheeks and shot him a warning glance. Too bad if he was uncomfortable about sharing an adventure with her. She wasn't about to let him start in about how he didn't want to be held responsible for her reputation or how her neighbors might talk. If she and Colt got arrested for sleeping on the beach, her neighbors wouldn't give a fig.

"I'm in on this, Montana man. Don't you dare try to talk me out of it."

"Okay, California girl." He eyed her as though she were Eve offering Adam the apple. "I'll go back to my hotel and change. You dig up the sleeping bags, and I'll meet you back here at ten. And wear your bathing suit under a pair of sweats. If we're going to break the law, we may as well rile some fish while we're at it."

After Colt left, Melanie tore into her room and searched for the camping equipment. She felt giddy, like a twelve-year-old on her first sleepover or a teenager preparing for an important date.

She showered, washed and dried her hair, dusted herself with peach-scented body powder and brushed her teeth. Next she dabbed on a little lip gloss and a couple strokes of waterproof mascara. A pair of tight black leggings, low-heeled boots and an oversize white sweatshirt completed her free-spirited look. By the time Colt returned, Melanie knew she was the picture of good health, her suntanned skin naturally glowing.

As usual, he managed to steal her breath. Attired in casual gray sweats and tennis shoes, his thick raven hair banded at his nape, he smelled like fresh-showered male. Spice aftershave and a trace of deodorized soap. The faint beard stubble shadowing his jaw hinted at danger. She found herself wondering how it would feel against her own skin.

His dark gaze took in her appearance in one standoffish sweep before he glanced down. "What's all this?"

Why was he always so guarded? she wondered. Was he that uncomfortable about his attraction to her, or did he view all women as the enemy? "A few things I thought we might need."

He eyed the overstuffed backpack. "Like what?"

"Towels, an extra blanket…you know, things." A portable radio, three flashlights, extra batteries, a first aid kit.

"And in there?" Colt pointed to another cloth bag.

Although her heart pounded like a bass drum, she tried to appear relaxed. She didn't want him to know how excited she was. She managed to shrug in nonchalance. "Food and water." Gourmet cheese, seasoned crackers, grapes, celery and carrot sticks, cherry tomatoes, ranch dressing, a big bottle of spring water, a thermos of hot chocolate, paper cups, plates, floral-printed napkins. Just a little midnight snack she happened to throw together.

Before he could comment on the lantern she had placed beside the sleeping bags, she spoke up. "The beach is dark at night."

"No kidding," he growled. "Let's go."

They gathered the supplies and headed to the stretch of beach directly across from her condo. "In case you decide you want to go home in the middle of the night," he said.

Not a chance, she thought, deliberately inhaling his enticing scent.

She lit the lantern while he spread the blanket on the sand

and weighted the opposite corners with the backpack and food supply. A slight breeze rippled the unanchored ends as he unrolled their sleeping bags and placed them on the blanket—as far apart from each other as possible, she noticed.

The beach was quiet but for the whispering wind and seductive lull of water rolling and foaming onto the shore. A bright moon bathed the sand and surf in a soft silver light. Stars winked from a crushed-velvet sky.

They both sat down and stared up at the heavens.

Awe sounded in Colt's voice. ''Makes you feel small, doesn't it?''

''But not insignificant,'' Melanie said.

He lowered his chin and turned toward her. The golden glow of the lantern illuminated his angular features, enhancing the hollow ridges beneath his cheeks and turning his eyes a shade lighter. They shimmered like her favorite root beer candy.

''No, not insignificant,'' he parroted. ''It makes you glad to be alive, to be a part of something so wondrous.''

She nodded. For her, the sky, the stars, the beach, couldn't compare to the wonder of this man, or to the knowledge that he had chosen her to carry his child, to bring forth another life.

They sat quietly then, staring at each other. A strand of hair blew across his lips like a raven feather, almost blue in its glossy black sheen. He pushed it away, toward the ponytail from which it had escaped.

As Melanie's own freshly washed hair fluttered around her face, a sense of vulnerability came over her. Every fiber of her being longed for this man—heart, body and soul.

Minutes, long and intense, passed before the sound of Colt's voice caressed the night air. ''Sometimes you remind me of someone I used to know…someone from a long time ago, before my life got so messed up.''

Melanie watched the strand of hair return to his lip, and all she could think about was kissing it away until the enormity of his words struck. *She reminded him of someone.*

''Who?'' she asked, fearing the pounding of her heart might give her away.

''Just a girl. Like I said, it was a long time ago.'' He sounded sorry for mentioning it, as though it were too personal to share. "I was just a kid. It doesn't matter."

It mattered to her. More than he could possibly know. "Was she a friend?"

"Sort of. It's hard to explain. I never even knew her last name or where she lived."

She had never expected her old self to surface, yet in some diminutive way it had. "Why do I remind you of her?"

His root beer gaze studied hers, as deeply as it could in the dim light. "Your eyes seem the same." His next words slipped out slowly as though emerging from the place where distant memories are stored, a place he hadn't visited in a very long time. "God, she was shy. So tiny…fragile, like a baby bird with a broken wing. You know, like she needed someone to protect her."

Melanie's eyes misted. Should she tell him? No, she couldn't. Not yet.

"Did you?"

The renegade piece of hair slipped into his mouth. This time he shoved it roughly behind his ear. "Did I what?"

"Protect her."

He shrugged. "I don't know. That era of my life is pretty vague, all that drinking eventually pickled some brain cells, I guess."

Melanie realized he was too humble to admit the truth. He had protected her and he darn well knew it.

He appeared to be gnawing the inside of his lip. "I'm not saying that you're fragile or anything like that." Apparently he realized what a sad picture he had painted of the girl she reminded him of. "I know how independent you are, and you're anything but shy. It's just your eyes, that's all. She had pretty eyes, like yours. Big and blue."

Melanie's chest heated. She felt as if her heart was made of wax and he'd just set the wick aflame. Clearly, eyes were the window to the soul, and even though Melanie had changed, the fragile little girl she had been still dwelled in her soul.

"What do you mean, I'm anything but shy?" she asked, trying to lighten Colt's mood. Reflections from the past hovered over him like a melancholy cloud.

He eyed her curiously before a smirk curled one corner of his lips. The crooked smile made him appear younger, a tad mischievous. "You invited yourself to sleep with me, California girl. That hardly constitutes shy."

True, she thought. Gertrude would have never done that. "So I'm sleeping with you, am I?"

A muscle in his jaw ticked. "Oh, hell. I did it again." He shook his head. "What can I say? It's the Freud thing. Subconsciously everything comes down to sex."

"Sex on the beach," Melanie supplied in a low, sultry tone, teasing him.

"That's quite an offer, California girl."

She laughed. It felt wonderful to possess the confidence to flirt with him. "It's a drink, Colt. Sex on the beach, that's what it's called."

"Yeah, I know." He removed his shoes and socks, then peeled off his sweatshirt and tossed it aside. "But it conjures up quite an image."

"What are you doing?" She focused on his nipples. They were erect.

He untied the white string on his pants. "Taking my clothes off."

Her voice quivered. "Why?"

Colt stood, and when he did, the sea breeze twirled sand at his feet. A copper silhouette in the moonlight, he mirrored a pagan god, fluid and long. "We're going swimming, remember?"

She glanced at the waves crashing onto the shore. The water looked dark and cold. Menacing.

When Colt began pushing his sweats down, Melanie realized she was kneeling before him in near worship, watching every breath he took, every primitive movement. As he leaned forward to rid himself of the fleece-lined garment, raw, powerful sinew bunched and stretched. The animal in him, she thought. Jungle cat sensuality.

He had a thin, dark line of hair below his navel. She knew

where it led, so she moistened her lips and allowed her curious gaze to follow it—right down to the swim trunks riding low on his hip.

Quickly her eyes shot back up to his face where one black eyebrow slanted in the opposite direction of a crooked smile.

"So, Melanie, are you going to undress or not?"

Was her swimsuit top white or silver? Between the lantern's amber haze and the moon's soft glow, he couldn't tell. What he could attest to was the shape and size of her breasts. And the condition. Her nipples were hard, flawless pearls reflecting light.

Colt dropped onto his haunches and watched her undress. He'd never watched a woman strip before. Not like this. The sand, the breeze, the smell of saltwater—it was all so erotic.

She slipped her boots off and then stood to remove her pants, just as he had done earlier. She discarded the snug leggings with such feminine grace he shuddered, a chill tingling his spine. Mesmerized, his gaze followed her hands down her body.

When the task was done, she weaved a little as though intoxicated by his hungry stare. Although he had admired her delicate figure through the slim-fitting fashions she wore, his imagination had done her a disservice. How could he ever have thought this woman too small? *You need to put some meat on those tiny bones of yours,* he'd told her. Well, he had been wrong.

Her slender curves boasted perfection: high, round breasts; a trim waist; flared hips; legs toned and taut; thighs smooth enough to caress a man yet strong enough to urge him to completion.

This bikini-clad female could haven been spawned from the ocean, an auburn-haired sea nymph, a sensuous creature with whom to share the elements.

"Come on!" He shot up, grabbed her hand and started pulling her toward the shore.

The water caressed him like cool fingers. He released her hand and let the swell crash over him. It lapped his legs, his waist, his chest. Colt reveled in the brisk cleansing, in the salt, the foam, the wet sand between his toes. For him, it felt like a baptism of sorts. Years of sin being washed away.

When the wave receded, Colt turned toward Melanie, expecting to see her expression resembling his.

What he saw disturbed him. She stood in her little bikini, shivering, her big blue eyes blinking away droplets of water. He'd been wrong about her not being fragile.

"I'm freezing," she said, teeth chattering.

Colt cursed himself. He should have predicted as much. She'd been away from the snow and sleet and crisp Montana winds far too long. A nocturnal California sea hardly compared, but to most it would seem cold.

Guilt washed over him. He should be protecting Melanie, not dragging her into the ocean at midnight. This woman had offered to host his seed, to cradle his baby in the warmth of her womb.

"I'm taking you home."

"No," she protested through chattering teeth. "I'll be fine once I dry off."

"Damn it, Melanie—"

His argument was quickly silenced by her "Oh, my God." Neither had noticed an enormous wave rising behind them until it started to descend. Immediately, Colt grabbed hold of Melanie and pulled her into his arms. Since she was at least a foot smaller than he, Colt struggled to keep her from being completely immersed in the vicious onslaught.

When the crisis ended and the water began moving away, catastrophe struck again. Melanie, still visibly shaken, stumbled against him and they both lost their footing and landed in the wet sand. Breaths caught and limbs tangled as they rolled and fell.

"Oh, my God," she said again, gripping his forearms. "That scared me."

"Yeah." Her proximity scared him more. She was on top of him, eye-to-eye, breast to chest, hip to hip.

They were both covered in wet sand and seaweed. This wasn't quite what he'd had in mind when he longed to become a part of the ocean. "We better go before another one comes."

Melanie righted herself, at least partially. Straddling his lap for balance, her body rocked intimately against his. Colt swallowed a frustrated groan.

"Something grabbed my foot," she said. "That's why I fell."

"What do you think it was?" he asked, barely grinding out the simple words, struggling to retain a modicum of dignity.

"I'm not really sure. Maybe an eel or an octopus. It felt slimy."

Colt noticed her teeth had quit chattering. "Seaweed probably. It's all over your legs."

"Oh."

Her smile made his groin throb even harder. She looked gorgeous in the moonlight, seaweed, sand and all. "Let's go." He pushed himself up and took her with him. Another wave was on its way.

He spied the faint, flickering light from their lantern and carried her toward it. Her legs were wrapped around his middle, her arms clinging to his neck.

"Where are you taking me?" she asked when he reached the campsite, grabbed a couple towels from the backpack and kept going.

"To the nearest shower."

She started shivering again but allowed him to turn on the outside shower along the cement walk that bordered the sand. The streetlights provided an incandescent glow so he held her just as she was, against his flesh, and let the water sluice over them. Soon he found himself running his hands through her hair, rinsing the sand out. When she returned the favor and released his debris-encrusted ponytail, he ducked his head under the cool water and sighed. They were like desperate lovers, wrapped in a tight embrace, their bodies humming with desire.

Colt gazed into Melanie's passion-glazed eyes. It would be so easy to kiss her. His tongue would seek entrance and they would devour each other with moist, carnal thrusts. Their tongues would imitate what their bodies craved.

Kissing her would be so damn easy. Yet so damn hard.

If he did it, their relationship would change, and that was a risk he wasn't prepared to take. Spontaneous sex had brought him nothing but trouble in the past. Women always seemed to want more. And he didn't have it to give. He didn't want to be the object of someone's misguided affection. Not ever again.

Colt eased Melanie to the ground, out of his arms. It was a painful separation. Her body had grazed his all the way down. Quickly he tossed her one of the towels he'd hitched over a bench.

They dried vigorously, looked at each other and sputtered into nervous laughter. It seemed to be the only way to ease the sexual tension.

"How does a warm, bubbly whirlpool sound?" she asked, wrapping the towel around herself.

"Like a good idea." He needed to get her stubborn little hide out of the cold, and if he didn't go with her, he knew she'd protest. Melanie's health was of grave importance. Soon his child would be taking nourishment from her. Once she conceived, he told himself for the upteenth time, this man-woman, hungry-for-each-other thing would pass. There would be no denying her role in his life then. She'd be his surrogate. A vehicle for his baby. Nothing more.

Melanie sank into the hot tub, luxuriating in the warmth while desperately trying to rationalize Colt's sudden aloofness. On the beach, he had handled her with such gentleness, such infinite care that she had felt like a precious gem from the sea—protected and treasured—admired beyond comprehension.

And that shower. Melanie knew Colt had contemplated kissing her. The way he'd moistened his own lips and stared at hers—there was no doubt in her mind how badly he wanted to sample her tongue, taste what would have brought them both such pleasure.

God help her, she wanted to taste him too, every virile, salty, ocean-dampened inch. His body had felt so right against hers, hard where hers was soft, narrow where hers flared. When she'd released Colt's ponytail and smoothed his tangled mane, he'd closed his eyes, allowing her an unobtrusive view of his body, of the water funneling from his hair onto his chest. It had traveled like mist from a waterfall, rippling between contracting abdominal muscles only to disappear into the cove that joined their hips.

Melanie stilled her thoughts and glanced over at Colt. He, too, was immersed in the steaming hot tub, and although his eyes were closed, his features were stoic. Where passion had once been so beautifully etched, apathy remained.

Damn him, she thought. One step forward. Two steps back. The man was exasperating. "Are you hungry?" she asked, slipping out of the tub. "I made some snacks for the beach. We may as well nibble on them now."

His eyes flew open, but he didn't respond. Instead he watched her walk across the balcony to retrieve the food bag. She smoothed her wet hair, wishing she knew how to saunter like a seductress. Her iridescent swimsuit could have been designed for an Egyptian queen. Cleopatra would have worn it well, and she would have known how to glide across the tile. Antony would have been panting at her feet by now.

Colt's dark eyes revealed nothing, not one trace of emotion. "I don't want anything," he said when Melanie sat on the edge of the tub, dipped her feet in and proceeded to peel the lids off several plastic containers.

"Suit yourself." She popped a cheese square into her mouth and flashed him a sickeningly sweet smile, feigning indifference to his irritating behavior.

When his eyes drifted closed, she opened a box of crackers and crinkled the paper. When that failed to rouse him, she crunched on a carrot stick, then another.

His eyes shot open just as she licked a dollop of ranch dressing from her fourth carrot.

Their gazes locked and she froze, suddenly self-conscious. His piercing stare was fixed on her lips. For a man who had refused food, he looked hungry. Downright ravenous, like he was on the verge of a ferocious attack, capable of devouring her entire mouth in one voracious swoop.

A more sexually experienced woman would have seized the moment, Melanie thought, done something provocative and enticing. But not her. She just sat there, immobile, too discomposed to know how to react.

"Are you trying to drive me crazy?" he asked in a voice rougher than the harshest sandpaper.

Did his question have dual meaning? "Excuse me?"

"You're making all kinds of noise."

"Sorry." She snaked her tongue out again, and licked the last dollop of dressing off the carrot, thinking that's probably what Cleopatra would have done. She had better learn pretty darn quick how to seduce a man. Once she was waddling around in maternity dresses it might be too late. She assumed part of the fun of falling in love was making love, something most couples experienced before pregnancy. Now that her relationship with Colt had progressed, artificial insemination didn't sound the least bit romantic.

"I better go." Dark and brooding as ever, Colt emerged from the tub, then grabbed a towel, which he hastily wrapped around his waist.

She gazed up at him and did her damnedest to appear unaffected by the moisture trailing down his body. The hair on his long, muscled legs glistened, and one tear-shaped droplet had captured one flat, brown nipple. Where he stood, water pooled at his feet.

Gorgeous. Stubborn. "Whatever, Colt."

"Yeah, whatever," he mimicked, unconsciously licking his bottom lip when she dipped her finger into the dressing. "It's been a long day. I'm tired."

She tasted the dip and shrugged. "I'd invite you to stay but I know how old-fashioned you are about such things. Besides, I could use a little time to myself." She tugged on the strap around her neck. "This bathing suit is getting uncomfortable. I'll probably just slip it off, then slide back into the water. There's nothing more soothing than being naked in a whirlpool."

He gulped the night air, released the towel around his waist and tossed it toward her. "Don't you dare catch cold."

Barely casting a glance in his direction, Melanie found the grapes and treated herself to one. "See ya, Montana man. You sleep tight."

The rustling sound of movement told her he was shoving his sweats on, right over his still-damp body. "I mean it, Melanie."

"Goodbye, Colt."

"I swear," he seethed in a low, uncontrolled voice, searching the balcony for his shoes, "if you get sick, I'll kill you."

Sexual frustration was written all over him. His eyes moved over her like flickering torches, and every time she sucked a grape into her mouth, he caught his breath. She forced back a smile. If his tennis shoes had been any closer, they would have jumped up and bitten him.

"I'm so touched that you care," she said, twisting the bikini tie around her neck as though intending to release it. Cleopatra would have been proud. Colt actually groaned.

He stumbled over his shoes, picked them up and cursed. A moment later he stomped off the balcony and into her house. From her vantage point, she could see him tearing out the front door, his exit creating a slight thud and deliberate rattle.

"I love you, Colt Raintree," she whispered, reaching for the towel he'd worn while staring at the water puddle he'd left behind. "And before the year is up, I pray you'll love me, too."

Six

Melanie placed the sketch pad on the coffee table. The person knocking on the cabin door must be Colt. Even though they had spent very little time together since returning to Montana last week, she figured he would visit today.

"Morning." His jeans were faded, boots dusty and shirt soiled, but she had never seen a more beautiful sight. She couldn't help but wonder if men like Colt had any idea how appealing their work-roughened appearance was. Almost every city girl she knew had some sort of secret cowboy fantasy.

"Hi. Come on in." She backed away from the door and watched as he passed. He had a loose-hipped gait. Long, lean and lethal. "Do you want to sit down?"

"No. I just stopped by to see if you're settled in all right," he said, gazing around the rustic interior of the cabin. "Compared to your condo, this place is pretty primitive."

"It suits me fine." The native-timber structure had wood floors, a stone fireplace, a faded Navaho area rug, wrangler-made furnishings and a view from every window: lush green pastures, rolling hills, tall pines. Melanie had turned the larger of the two rustic bedrooms into her studio. Luckily it had plenty of natural light.

"The kitchen is small," he said. "The bathroom, too."

"I'm only one person."

"Yeah." He adjusted his Stetson out of what seemed like habit, then reached into his pocket and held out a key. "It's to the main house. You're welcome to use it anytime you want. You know, in case you ever feel like cooking a big meal or something."

Melanie nibbled on her smile. Apparently Colt craved some home-cooked meals. For a man who wanted to raise a baby on his own, he was a bit of a chauvinist where food preparation and women were concerned.

She accepted the key. Colt's chauvinism just might work in her favor. As the saying went: The way to a man's heart is through his stomach. "Thanks. I really do like to experiment with new recipes. And this kitchen is a bit old-fashioned." She glanced back at the cast-iron stove, which in truth she found charming. "The one in the main house has everything an amateur chef could need."

He nodded, shifted his stance, then asked, "Are you getting a lot of work done?"

She spied her empty sketch pad. "Not really, how about you?"

"Not much, I suppose. There's more horses to be shod."

"Don't you have someone who comes out to do that?" She knew that much about ranch life. Equine vets and farriers made regular rounds.

"I prefer to handle it on my own. My grandfather was a blacksmith by trade. He taught me what I needed to know."

"That's good." Melanie exhaled, wondering when Colt was going to say what was really on his mind. Of course, she thought she knew but decided to let him bring it up. "Are you sure you don't want to sit down? I made a fresh pot of coffee. You know I grind my own beans."

A grin split across his handsome face. "Sure. Okay."

He headed for the rough-hewn sofa while she made her way

into the tiny kitchen. She knew Colt appreciated the gourmet coffees she had introduced him to in California.

"Almond mocha," Melanie said, handing him the strong brew in a stoneware cup. The old-fashioned kitchen was equipped with copper pots and a matched set of stone-laden dishes.

"Thanks." He sipped the coffee then looked up. "Aren't you having any?"

She shook her head, smoothed her denim dress, sat down in the curved-back chair near the fireplace, and crossed her legs. "One morning jolt of caffeine is enough for me." She decided not to explain that she brewed a full pot every morning because she liked the aroma.

Colt placed the clay-colored cup on the end table beside the couch. "Are you nervous about tomorrow?"

Finally. The true reason for his visit. The scheduled insemination. "A little," she said, thinking she was a basket case. After tomorrow there would be no turning back. Morning sickness, weight gain, labor. What woman wouldn't feel anxious about pregnancy?

He offered a weak smile, not much in the way of comfort. "Can you plan on being ready by nine? I'd like to be early."

Nine? Her appointment wasn't until eleven. The last thing she wanted to do was sit around in the doctor's waiting room while her stomach did cartwheels. "You don't have to take me. I can drive myself over."

"Be kind of foolish to take two cars," he said, as though her preference didn't count. "I'll pick you up at nine."

Stubborn male arrogance, she thought. "You might as well stay here tomorrow and get some work done. Like you said, there's lots of horses to be shod. I don't need you to go with me."

He cocked an eyebrow. "Yes, you do."

Melanie let out a irritated "tsk" followed by a equally irritated sigh. She was certainly capable of getting herself to the doctor on time. Did he think she was going to change her mind and hightail it back to the coast? Besides, the whole thing was somewhat embarrassing. Much too personal. She didn't want to face him right after it was done. "Honestly, Colt—"

"Melanie, I have to go."

She gazed at him curiously before realization dawned and her entire face flamed. Oh, God. Talk about embarrassing. Of course Colt had to be there. The procedure required his sample. Without him…

She toyed with a button on her dress. "I'll be ready by nine."

"Good. Fine." He stood up to leave, and she noticed his dark skin looked a little flushed, too.

The following morning nine o'clock came too soon. Melanie had changed her clothes three times before settling on her favorite faded blue jeans, a simple white blouse, a brown tooled-leather belt and a pair of Tony Lamas to match. She'd curled her hair and applied a cream concealer beneath her eyes. She hadn't slept a wink. Well, maybe a wink. Sometime in the wee hours of the morning, she'd dozed off, only to be jarred back to life by a screeching alarm clock.

Melanie stared at the man standing in the doorway. He wore jeans, too, and brown boots. A pale-blue Western shirt complemented his bronzed complexion and a trophy buckle rode low on his narrow hips. Midnight hair flowed over wide shoulders.

Handsome as ever.

He held out a small bouquet of fresh-picked wildflowers. The colorful posies looked delicate in his large, callused hand. "For a pretty lady," he said.

She blinked back tears. Today, of all days, she needed flowers, needed to feel appreciated as a woman. The scheduled procedure had her feeling like a scientific specimen.

"Thank you." She accepted the gift and brushed the petals against her cheek, inhaling their scent. Incense from the earth—fresh, sweet and clean. "I'll put them in some water, then we can be on our way."

She clipped a bluebell into the gold barrette that secured one side of her hair and arranged the bouquet in an antique copper vase.

"I'm ready."

They climbed into his Chevy Suburban and strapped in. Her red convertible rested in the three-car garage. As much as Colt had argued with her that the vintage Mustang belonged in storage in California, she'd had it brought to Montana, anyway. "I'll lease you a nice, new, safe truck," he'd said. "A four-wheeler that won't get stuck in the snow. These country roads are brutal. Half of them aren't even paved."

What could she have said to him? That she didn't want to go back to California? That she hoped to make Bluff Creek Ranch her permanent residence? "I like my car" had been her response.

Unfortunately they hadn't gotten along well their last few days in California, and once they returned to Montana, Colt all but ignored her. Luring him into a body-painting session had been next to impossible. "I don't want to think about that nonsense until after the insemination," he'd told her. She had stewed for days over his flippant attitude. Her artwork was hardly nonsense.

Melanie touched the flower in her hair as Colt maneuvered the vehicle down a narrow, winding road. Her perfect man had his flaws, but she loved him nonetheless.

He glanced over. "I'm sure we have time to grab some breakfast. We could stop by the diner, if you'd like."

Mountain Mabel's, the country diner. Bittersweet nostalgia washed over her. As teenagers, she and Gloria had spent many an afternoon there, sipping cherry colas and whispering secrets. "How about lunch instead? I'm not really hungry right now."

"Okay."

They rode in silence the rest of the way, each lost in thought. Colt's ranch was on the outskirts of town, thirty rough miles from the medical center. When they finally arrived, it was 10:00 a.m.

As they entered the building through the double glass doors, Melanie's stomach decided to growl, much too loudly.

Colt glanced her way but didn't comment until they neared the elevator and her stomach rumbled again. He raised an eyebrow. "I thought you weren't hungry."

She pushed the button and eyed the other people gathering near the elevator. She'd skipped dinner last night and breakfast this morning. "I'm just a little too nervous to eat," she whispered.

The elevator door opened, apparently stilling a response from Colt. He ushered Melanie in behind two elderly women and a uniformed lab technician. No one spoke in the elevator, including Colt. As soon as he and Melanie exited on their designated floor, she looked for the ladies' room. "I need to splash some water on my face," she told him.

When she emerged from the rest room, he took her hand, then cocked his head in a concerned gesture. "You're trembling, Melanie. Are you that nervous or don't you feel well?"

"I…" How could she explain the range of emotions rioting within her? She's the one who had called him, offering to be his surrogate. Why would a surrogate be anxiety ridden because the father-to-be wasn't in love with her, and the procedure made her feel like a rented womb?

No, she couldn't reveal all of her trauma, but she could at least explain part of it. "I've never been comfortable in doctors' offices," she said, glancing down the hallway. "When I first went into foster care, I was kind of sickly. Pale and anemic. I had to get vitamin shots regularly…"

Melanie fidgeted with the flower in her hair. "As hard as it had been living with my mom, she was still my mom. Going to live with strangers was frightening. And then on top of it all, I was sick. Although my first foster mother provided adequate care, she wasn't particularly loving. At the time I felt as though my condition was a burden to her, like the doctor visits were a nuisance."

She glanced up and met Colt's sympathetic gaze, suddenly feeling foolish and a little guilty about her admission. She had spent more time in doctors' offices than he could possibly know. For a time, hospitals and doctor's visits were part of her daily routine. She had hairline scars to prove it. "Look, I don't usually get so weird about going to the doctor. It's not as if I'm neurotic or anything…it's just this procedure. "

Colt touched her hair, then the side of her face. "What about it, Melanie?"

His touch brought on an unbearable ache, a need for compassion. She hadn't expected the insemination to trigger her insecurities to such a degree. "Creating life should be joyous, but this procedure is so cold and clinical. I feel lonely, like I did when I was a kid."

His hand drifted from her cheek to her shoulder, then slid down her back, where he drew circular motions with his fingertips. "Tell me what to do. How can I help?"

Tears sprang to her eyes as she leaned into him and clutched his shirt. Quickly he enveloped her in warmth, the strong embrace tripling her need. She raised on her toes, buried her face in his hair and pressed her lips to his ear. "I want you to kiss me," she whispered.

Colt's sharp exhale vibrated his chest. "I will," he said in a quiet, husky voice, turning his head. "But not here, there's people…"

Melanie followed his sight down the hall. There were men and women, probably other patients, coming toward them. "Where?"

A smile touched his lips, just slightly. "How about the stairwell? No one uses the stairs in these kind of buildings. Too many stories."

"All right."

When he took her hand and led her to the other end of the hallway, to the door leading to the stairs, she felt a tad wicked, as though they were headed to a secret rendezvous.

"How's this?" he asked.

Melanie looked around. The walls were industrial gray, the stairs cement, the white paint on the metal rail chipping in spots. Drab as the setting was, there was not one sign of life. She was alone with Colt, the man who had just agreed to kiss her.

Suddenly this quiet stairwell was the most beautiful place on earth and the most fragrant. Colt's spicy cologne and her floral perfume formed an enticing aroma.

"Perfect," she said.

They stood on the small slab of cement above the first step and faced each other. Colt reached out and cupped her chin with both hands, then leaned forward and kissed her forehead, each eyebrow and the tip of her nose. He even kissed her checks with his eyelashes, fluttered them like butterfly wings. When he finally settled his mouth over hers and pressed gently, Melanie closed her eyes.

How many years had she dreamed of this, of feeling his lips worship hers? That's what he was doing, she decided, as his lips moved over hers with excruciating tenderness. The velvety contact was too chivalrous to be considered anything but reverent.

She basked in him, in his texture, his taste, in the man he'd become, in the boy he once was. They were both there, exploring her for the first time, a teenage boy teaching an innocent girl to kiss, a man coaxing a woman, praising without words.

It ended too soon. He moved back to look at her. They hadn't caressed, hadn't opened their mouths or teased each other with their tongues, but the exchange had been deep. Filled with emotion.

"We should go," he said, his voice vibrating as though stunned by the intensity of the kiss, chaste as it had been.

She nodded and followed him to the door. As he turned the knob, she caught his attention.

"Colt?"

He turned back around. "Hmm?"

"Thank you."

Colt's being filled with wonder. Not one female in all his thirty-two years had ever seemed more grateful for his touch.

"I should be thanking you," he said. "For the baby…"

She smiled, and his heart clenched in a cross between pain and joy, an emotion so foreign he couldn't quite fathom it. And then, as though her smile had bewitched him, Colt lifted his thumb to her mouth, to touch it, to feel the magic.

Soft, he thought, as he began moving his thumb, stroking gently, the way a man without sight would explore. "So sweet," he found himself saying, recalling the taste of a kiss only moments ago he had struggled to contain.

Her lips parted, and Colt battled his next breath. Air, hot and heavy, escaped his lungs and brushed her cheek, stirring a strand of auburn hair that fell across the flower he had given her. *Wildflowers.* He hadn't planned to pick them, but when he strode across the ranch this morning and saw them swaying in the sunshine, he acted on impulse. Now the memory of each dewy petal aroused him, just like moisture between Melanie's parted lips.

Unable to control the heat pooling low in his body, he pushed the side of his thumb into her mouth, against her teeth. His caress no longer gentle, he lost himself in her spell, in the hard white teeth that nipped him curiously. Almost mischievously.

She gazed up at him through blue eyes sparked with passion, and he realized her tongue was moving over his thumb.

Damn it, he thought, watching her suckle his flesh. *This wasn't supposed to happen.*

He jerked his hand away, intending to cease their contact, but grabbed her wrists instead and aggressively pushed her against the wall beside the door.

He felt as though two animals had emerged. The one, dangerously male, battled hunger while the other, the weaker one, submitted herself as prey, encouraging him to quell his desire.

Colt lifted her hands in the air and pressed her arms to the wall. As he pinned her in place, he decided which gender was the weaker sex. Though sweet and soft and innocent, she managed to render him helpless to her charm.

"Kiss me," he rasped. "I kissed you, now it's your turn to kiss me."

"Come closer," she beckoned, freeing herself from his grasp.

He did as she bade and lowered his head. She wrapped her arms around his neck and brushed his aroused sex with the soft sway of her hips. He bent his knees, caught her hips, and pulled her even closer so he could nestle between her thighs, cradle himself in her femininity.

God help me, he thought as her mouth covered his.

First she nibbled his bottom lip in a playful bite, then bathed it with her tongue. He sipped her tongue as it darted out, before his determined thrust plundered her mouth and pillaged like a greedy marauder.

This kiss was reckless, as turbulent as the wrath of Mother Earth. Hunger whirled like a tornado of pent-up passion, drawing them into its swirling circle. Tongues probed and mated in a rhythm so seductive it went beyond his conception of kiss. They were making love—with their mouths. Each thrust delved deeply, stoking embers into wet, hot flames.

Colt fell deeper into her mouth, into her warmth, into the carnal pleasure she provided. The delicious sighs and moans issuing from her throat were too much to bear. On a groan, he went on a quest—of her body. First, he explored her rib cage where he examined every feminine bone. So tightly was her body pressed to his that he felt as though she had actually been created from his rib, her tiny frame formed from his.

As he continued his exploration, the kiss gentled and they came up for air. She closed her eyes and he watched her. Watched her lips curl into a satisfied smile, watched the aroused flush on her cheeks deepen as he pleasured her with his touch, teased her through her clothes. And when she purred and her nipples pebbled beneath his thumbs, it took every ounce of control he possessed to keep from tearing off her blouse and lowering his head.

Take her home, he told himself. *Carry her to bed. Sate your desire, spill your seed. Make her pregnant.*

If he did, what would happen afterward? Would she want to be part of his life? Would she confuse sex with love? Would the baby become *theirs* instead of *his?* Or would she walk away and leave him feeling empty? Would he crave her on long, cold nights, only to wake up alone? Hell, he was human after all, and it was possible he'd miss her companionship. He liked Melanie. A lot. Maybe too much.

When his caressing ceased, Melanie opened her eyes and they stared at each other. He knew she saw the question in his gaze, the wage of his mental war.

"Colt—"

He stilled her words with the tap of his finger to her kiss-swollen lips. "Don't say it." *Don't offer yourself to me. Don't encourage me to lose control.*

"You have an appointment," he said, eyeing her beautifully tousled appearance with a painful grimace. "And it's time to go."

Mountain Mabel's looked the same: faded red booths covered with vinyl tablecloths, knotty-pine walls and a thin layer of sawdust sprinkled on the floor. Even Mable hadn't changed all that much. Her pink uniform still stretched across ample hips and her gray-streaked hair still resembled a helmet. Apparently the woman wasn't concerned about the ozone layer; her brand of aerosol hairspray was anything but environment-friendly. Melanie assumed Mable stored cases of the discontinued stuff in her basement.

"Colt Raintree." Mable stood, order book and pencil in hand. "How are you?"

He flashed a charming smile. "Craving some of your beef stew."

"You got it." She turned to Melanie with blatant curiosity. "And your lady friend?"

Melanie's smile twitched. Clearly Mable wondered who Colt's lady friend was. *It's me—Gertrude, remember? The skinny kid with braces?*

"A turkey sandwich on wheat. And an iced tea," Melanie said.

"Coming right up." Mable paused then sauntered off, sliding Colt a sideways glance as she did.

"You'd think you were having lunch with an alien," Melanie said, gazing around the diner. Several pairs of eyes were fixed on her and Colt. One frosty blue pair belonged to an attractive blonde seated just across the aisle.

Although he shrugged indifferently, Melanie noticed he avoided the blonde's piercing stare. "I haven't been seen with a woman in a while."

Melanie stole another glance at the blonde. She had fluffy, shoulder-length hair and a lean body that looked as though it had been tailor-made for the embroidered Western blouse and crisp jeans she wore. A former rodeo queen, Melanie decided.

When Mable reappeared, she placed Melanie's iced tea on the table and poured Colt a cup of coffee. She lingered for a moment, apparently hoping for an introduction. Finally, Colt obliged. "Mable, this is Melanie Richards. She lived in Mountain Bluff for a short time but moved away to go to college."

The woman responded in kind to Melanie's "hi" then asked, "So, are you visiting, dear, or have you come back to stay?"

"I plan on being around for a while."

"That's nice," Mable said, slipping Colt another one of her not-too-subtle glances, to which he flashed a disarming smile. Apparently rumors about Colt's plans to hire a surrogate had been surfacing for some time. "Good to meet you, Melanie, enjoy your stay. And feel free to stop in anytime."

"Thanks. I will."

Colt appeared unaffected by Mable's curiosity. Clearly he was used to the gossip that surrounded him and took it in stride. When the waitress left, he gazed over at Melanie. "Do you feel any different?" he asked teasingly, grin in place.

From what? she wondered. His seed or his earth-shattering kiss? No wonder Colt Raintree still managed to stir up gossip. Devilishly handsome, he could charm a snake out of its skin. The man had a rakish brand of charisma.

She felt different all right. Deeper in love. "Like, am I going to order pickles and ice cream for dessert?"

His grin widened. "Now that it's done, I feel like a kid on Christmas eve. Only I have to wait nine months to unwrap my present."

Suddenly awed, Melanie touched her tummy.

Colt peered over the table and watched her. "Did you know that just a few hours after conception human cells start to form? There might be life happening inside you already."

When she looked up, their gazes locked and something too intimate to describe passed between them. The admiration in his eyes and the tenderness in his smile told her how blessed he felt.

For the third time that day, Melanie fell in love all over again. A driving need to know everything about him emerged. "Colt, I was wondering about your dad. Since he wasn't in your life, how did you end up with his last name?"

"Even though my grandparents weren't too happy about it, my mom insisted on it," he said. "I guess she thought she loved Toby Raintree and wanted her son to carry his name. Maybe the guy had swept her off her feet...but love? No way. She was too young."

Inwardly Melanie disagreed. She was living proof of a teenager who had fallen in love. "Your mom's story is tragic. Caring for a man she couldn't keep, not getting to see her son grow up."

"Yeah. I talk to her sometimes, in my prayers. I figure she's with my daughter, so they're both okay."

Colt never ceased to amaze her. Moody and wild yet so sensitive—a man who didn't realize how big his heart was or how much love it was capable of.

Mable returned with lunch. Colt's hearty stew came with a basket of warm bread and pads of butter. Melanie's sandwich had a side of coleslaw. "Thanks," they both said simultaneously.

He buttered a slice a bread, then dipped it into the stew. Melanie decided to take mental inventory of his favorite foods. She intended to cook for this man, hold him at night, know him as deeply as possible.

"Colt, do you wonder about your dad? Like where he is or if he has any other kids?"

He responded between mouthfuls. "Funny you should ask, because after I sobered up, I went on this personal quest, searching for my roots, trying to fit in somewhere. I didn't find my dad, but I met some nice folks at the reservation. They taught me some things about the Cheyenne Nation, cultural beliefs that helped get me through the rough times."

"Would it be proper to talk about them?" Melanie asked, uncertain of Native American protocol.

"Some things are." He sipped his coffee, then offered an explanation. "But you know, it was the simple things that helped the most. For instance, after my daughter died, there was a part of me that felt I hadn't mourned her properly, that I owed her something more."

Melanie kept silent and waited for him to continue, knowing how important this was to him.

"When I learned some of the Cheyenne practices for mourning, I realized that I needed to respect my daughter in the tra-

dition of the old ways. Cheyenne women used to cut their hair
short when a loved one died. And the men would unbraid their
hair and let it hang loose." He fingered a strand of his dark
mane. "I decided then that I would always keep my hair long.
I braid it now and then, but for a time I didn't. Leaving my hair
loose was my Cheyenne gift to Meagan."

He was such a good, caring man, Melanie thought. The kind
of man meant to be a father. "Are there any traditions for babies?"

He nodded, smiled. "There's an ear piercing ceremony. But
in some cases, the ears aren't actually pierced until later. At this
gathering, the person invited to pierce the baby's ears would just
make the motions." He touched his own earlobe where a tiny
silver hoop glistened. "It's said that if a father has his child's
ears pierced without ceremony, then he has no affection for that
child."

Melanie didn't need to ask Colt if he planned on having their
baby's ears ceremonially pierced. She could see by his expression that he would follow that tradition.

He swallowed another bite of stew. "You know, in the old
days, a well-crafted cradle was considered quite important. And
since you mentioned decorating the baby's room with an antique
cradle, I was thinking maybe we could search for one at some
of the Indian auctions."

"That's a great idea." Thrilled at the prospect of decorating
the nursery, Melanie planned to continue their conversation on
the same vein, but didn't get the chance. The lean blonde with
the icy blue eyes excused herself from her female companion
and glided over to their table.

"Raintree," she meowed, tossing a bleached yellow wave
over her shoulder. "Long time no see."

He eyed her with an aloof stare. "Susan, we're having
lunch."

"Me, too. I just wanted to say hello." Susan scooted in next
to him without blinking an eye. "I've missed you."

Colt's shoulders tensed. "Been busy."

Melanie's stomach fell. No doubt about it, Susan was one of
Colt's former lovers. And now that she was up close and per-

sonal, Melanie decided blondie didn't have enough class to have ever been crowned rodeo queen. More than likely, Susan procured her fame as a buckle bunny, a rodeo circuit groupie who serviced cowboys, then flashed the men's trophy buckles as if to say, "Look who I slept with."

Susan lifted her chin. "Colt and I are old friends," she said to Melanie.

"Real old," Colt interjected, an apology in his eyes. "Susan and I used to get drunk together."

The blonde laughed. "As I recall, Raintree, we had some good times."

"Really?" He looked her way. "Guess I must have been too plastered to remember them."

Melanie forced back a humiliating tear. Whether he had been drunk or not, he'd still bedded Susan, something he'd refrained from doing with her today. They had kissed and touched and nearly driven each other to the brink of madness, yet Colt had led her to the doctor's office instead of taking her home to conceive their child. Soon she would be thinking of herself as an oddity—a pregnant virgin.

Blondie bristled from Colt's last comment. "People have been talking about you, Raintree. They say you plan on having a kid with some stranger."

"I'm having a baby with a friend," he shot back, then turned to look at Melanie, his harsh tone softening. "Probably the best friend I've ever had."

Melanie gazed back at Colt and extended her hand toward Susan. She wasn't about to be intimidated by some bed-hopping bimbo, especially not after what Colt had just implied. "I'm Melanie Richards. Colt and I are new friends."

Susan shook Melanie's hand without missing a beat. "Well, then I suppose congratulations are in order," she said, icicles dripping from each word. "Pity Colt doesn't know how to have fun anymore. I'm sure you two will get along famously." She stood and fluffed her hair. "See ya round, Raintree."

Susan motioned to her companion at the table and the two strode by, each proudly displaying some indiscriminating cowboy's buckle.

"I'm sorry," Colt said to Melanie. "My past isn't pretty."

"Am I what you said?" she asked. The best friend he'd ever had?

"Yes, California girl, I do believe you are."

Seven

"You're spoiling that horse."

Melanie turned around so fast, Cinnamon nearly mistook her finger for a carrot.

Figures. Shorty, with that eagle-eyed look of his. "I...ah..." Dang that old man, anyway. Every time he glanced in her direction, which was often, her heart tried out for the Olympics. A hundred beats per minute. "Cinnamon looks forward to her treats."

"She'll start acting up when you're gone," he said, dusting his hands on his jeans. "Be expecting sugar cubes and carrots all the time. And I won't have time to be hand-feeding some fussy mare."

Melanie wanted to shoot him an I-plan-on-sticking-around-so-quit-complaining look but thought better of it. Shorty was the one person capable of causing trouble. It was just too early to tell Colt who she was, and if this sour old man figured it out...

"I'll ease up on the treats," she said, glancing away. She'd just have to sneak them to Cinnamon when Shorty was working the other side of the ranch.

"How come you never look me in the eye?" he asked, shifting his weight. "Can't trust someone who don't look ya in the eye. Usually means they got something to hide."

Wonderful. Now he was even more suspicious. "The FBI isn't looking for me. I'm not a drug dealer, a mobster or a terrorist," she retorted, staring straight at him. "I'm just an artist from California. And I didn't know hand-feeding horses was a crime." She spun on her Cuban-heeled boots. "Now, if you'll excuse me, I have work to do. I'm designing a wildlife series for a stationery line. Real untrustworthy stuff."

"Now, you hold on just a minute, girlie. I got me a thing or two to say."

Melanie kicked up a layer of dust on the barn floor. "What?" she snapped, facing him like an insolent child.

"Hey!"

Colt's harsh voice startled Melanie as much as it did Shorty. They both stood perfectly still and waited for his reprimand, their eyes widening. Somehow Colt had entered the barn without their knowledge. A little trick he must have picked up from his Cheyenne ancestors, Melanie decided.

"What the hell is going on?" he asked, his gaze darting between the guilty parties.

Melanie spoke first. "Nothing." Why couldn't she have just held her tongue? Shorty didn't deserve to be punished for her guilt. She did have something to hide. Her identity, her hope that Colt would fall in love with her.

"Nothing?" Colt parroted in apparent frustration. "Sure as hell sounded like something to me." He turned to Shorty. "Well?"

The old man removed his hat and smoothed the few gray hairs he still had left. Melanie thought he looked like scruffy boy facing the school principal, uncomfortable and fidgety, yet respectful.

"It was my doing," Shorty said. "The young lady's been bringing Cinnamon treats. I scolded her for it." He gazed at Melanie. "My apologies, ma'am."

"Apology accepted." She tugged on the points of her denim vest, thinking how childish she felt. "I'm sorry, too."

Shorty nodded and plopped his hat back on. "I'll just go about my business, then."

"Fine." Colt watched the old man saunter off. "Melanie, how about you and I go for a walk?"

She took a deliberate step back toward Cinnamon's curious nose. The horse sniffed her hair and Melanie reached up behind her to pat the mare's neck. "Are you going to yell at me, too?" she asked. Colt's sexy pout looked a tad vicious.

"No." The pout quirked into a lazy smile. "I just want to talk."

What woman in her right mind would refuse that smile? "Okay."

They left the barn and strode alongside the roping arena. Colt wore a pair of distracting fawn-colored chaps. Melanie considered walking behind him. A man in chaps was an admitted weakness, and Colt's taut, blue-jeaned butt looked exceptionally good, cupped between the rough leather.

He stopped and leaned against the fence. "How are you feeling?" he asked, studying her hair as it blew across her cheek.

In other words, did she feel pregnant? It had been two weeks since the insemination. "Fine. It's a bit early, I suppose. I'm not sick or anything."

"Yeah, too early," he agreed. "But damn if this waiting isn't driving me crazy."

"I know." As Melanie climbed onto the first fence rail, Colt grasped her waist to help her up. She settled her bottom against the wood, but he remained standing, tall and wicked in his slim-fitting chaps.

The lines around his mouth tightened and she assumed he was going to make an admission. She had come to recognize his expressions.

"I can't say I remember much about my wife's first trimester. I hadn't been overly involved in the early stages of her pregnancy," he said. "At eighteen, I was too busy mourning the loss of my freedom to consider her feelings. Marrying a girl I barely liked, let alone loved, was making me ill every morning." He shook his head. "Served me right, I suppose. I had no business sleeping with her in the first place."

Melanie tucked her windblown hair behind her ears. "Planned parenthood is easier, right?"

"Yeah." He laughed. "But I'll probably throw up this time, too. You know, sympathy pains or whatever they call it."

"You'd do that for me?" she asked with a teasing smile.

He lowered his chin and looked up beneath the brim of his hat. "Aw, shucks, ma'am, it ain't nothing, not fer a purty little thing like you."

Melanie reached over and pushed the Stetson farther down on his head, shielding his eyes completely. "Cowboys."

In a flash the cowboy in question stood in front of her, between her knees. The top fence rail put her at a slightly higher level than him, but his towering height presented a gorgeous view.

He tapped the underside of his hat, lifting it back up. Just as he unveiled his mischievous gaze, a grin twitched one corner of his lips, making him look a little like Elvis. "Admit it, California girl, you've got a thing for cowboys."

She looked down and found herself undressing him with her eyes: peeling a T-shirt off, flipping a buckle open, unzipping suede chaps, releasing blue jeans buttons. "Just one," she said, her voice breathy.

He moved closer. "How about Indians?"

She skimmed her fingers across his whiskered jaw. "What do you think?" she asked, the question slipping out in a near whisper.

"I think this is a dangerous game." He shuddered, caught her hand and pressed it tight against his face. "One we shouldn't play."

His actions defied his words. The hand that held hers tightened its grip. Dangerous or not, he wanted to be touched. "We're just flirting, Colt."

"That's all?"

"Yes." For now, she thought. Later she hoped there would be more.

He smiled and released her hand, apparently trying to lighten his mood. "Flirting is harmless," he said.

"And perfectly normal," she reassured.

Colt backed away and leaned against the fence rail once again, resuming a safe place beside her. Both stared straight ahead as a light breeze rippled over them. When the silence seemed to intensify their heartbeats, he interrupted it.

"I'm sorry about what happened between you and Shorty. He's a stubborn old man."

"I can be stubborn, too."

Colt turned to look at her. "Yeah, but I think Shorty is taking little things out on you because he doesn't approve of our situation."

"You mean the baby?"

"Not the baby as much as how I set out to get it. He thinks people who have babies together should be married."

Maybe old Shorty wasn't such a bad guy after all. "You can't blame him for being old-fashioned. He's from that generation."

"I know, but sometimes I think he's trying to direct my life because of the tragedy in his own. Believe it or not, the old guy was in love once. I mean, really in love. She died a couple years after they were married and they never had any kids. So, he's been pretty much alone for a long time."

Suddenly Melanie's heart ached for the elder cowboy. "That's so sad. Can you imagine how lonely he is?"

"Yeah, I can," Colt answered. "That's why this baby is so important to me. I just wish I could make him understand that."

A need to heal, to create balance and harmony immersed her soul like a balm. Melanie believed in happily-ever-afters. "Colt, do you think if we invited Shorty to go to the fair with us, he'd accept?"

His eyes widened. "We're going to the fair?"

She nodded. "It opens next week. I thought we could take Gloria's kids with us. I'm sure she and Fred would love a day off."

Colt laughed. "You and me, eight rambunctious kids and a grumpy old man? This I've got to see."

There were only five rambunctious kids, the other three thought they were too old to walk around the fair with "baby-sitters," so consequently, were allowed to roam the festivities unchaperoned. And convincing the grumpy old man to join them had been like pulling teeth from a rhino. Prune-faced, he shuffled along in his dusty boots, holding Joey Carnegie's hand. The four-year-old had decided the lanky ranch hand was grandpa material.

The other Carnegie siblings, two sets of twins, had chosen their favorite adult, as well. Sandy and Sarah, three minutes apart and identical in appearance, vied for Colt's attention. The six-year-old freckled blondes giggled uncontrollably every time he mixed their names up.

Melanie noticed Cory and Steven, fraternal twins who looked quite different, didn't seem to mind walking along with her. The nine-year-olds thought skateboarders and surfers from California were "pretty cool." Melanie lacked the courage to tell them she was neither.

"Time to eat," Colt said. "I'm starving."

"I want to go on the Ferris wheel again," little Joey whined.

"Can we get red candy apples?" one of the female twins asked, displaying a gap where her front teeth should have been.

"I want caramel!" her sister exclaimed, front teeth missing as well.

Colt examined the toothless grins with an arched eyebrow. "How about cotton candy instead? After we eat some real food."

"Come on!" Joey tugged Shorty toward the Ferris wheel line.

"All right, son." The older man looked back at Colt and Melanie. "We'll meet you at the burger stand."

Melanie shook her head and Colt laughed. "Talk about spoiling someone. He's indulged that kid's every whim," she said, secretly pleased. Sour-faced as Shorty appeared, she suspected he enjoyed the little boy's affection.

They ordered hot dogs, hamburgers and bushels of fries, then scooted into an empty picnic bench. Sandy and Sarah insisted Colt sit between them. He peered over at Melanie and grinned. She returned his smile, thinking she had never seen his brown eyes so bright.

The boys quarreled about who got more French fries while slurping noisily on their milkshakes. Melanie decided she wanted more than one child. Feisty as the siblings were with each other, they shared a special brand of love.

When one of the girls spilled ketchup down the front of her green blouse, Colt wiped it off, then stared at the faint stain. "What's your name?" he asked her.

"Sandy."

"Great. Now I can tell you apart. I think your mom must have dressed you alike just to drive me crazy."

With a devilish light in her eyes, Sandy peeked over at her sister. Sarah nodded to her twin as though a silent language had been conveyed, then deliberately squeezed ketchup onto her blouse and wiped it off, leaving a similar stain. Both girls pealed into laughter as Colt's head ping-ponged between them.

"Why you little pixies," Colt said, winking at Melanie.

Shorty and Joey showed up just then, stuffing hot dogs in their mouths as they strolled over. The older man shooed the child onto the bench seat and met Melanie's gaze. They stared at each other over the commotion at the table and the activity of the fair. Shorty swallowed his last bite and sat down.

She could swear a quick, faint smile had just twitched the elderly rancher's mustache. And all day long, he'd been watching her and Colt as though taking mental notes on their behavior. Did he approve of what he'd observed?

"Where to?" Colt asked the gang at the table.

"Cotton candy!" came one youthful reply.

"Petting zoo," was another.

"Let's try to win some prizes."

"Yeah!"

Colt smoothed his hair. "Okay. How about this? We'll get some cotton candy first, then go to the petting zoo and get eaten alive by baby goats and—"

Joey gasped. "The goats are gonna eat us?"

Colt responded on a chuckle. "No, tiger, they're going to eat our clothes. Goats nibble on anything they can get their mouths on."

"Maybe we better not go to the petting zoo," the boy said with a serious expression. "I don't want to walk around with no clothes on."

His brothers and sisters laughed as the adults exchanged a smile between them. "They won't eat our clothes off, Joey," Colt explained. "Just chew a little. And if we buy some goat treats for them to munch on, they'll probably leave our clothes alone."

"We'll buy lots of goat treats," Joey decided, fingering his striped T-shirt.

Colt nodded and continued planning the agenda. Melanie watched him through adoring eyes, thinking what a terrific father he was going to make, then caught herself looking up at the heavens, apologizing to Colt's daughter. *He probably was a terrific father,* she corrected, *and will be again.*

When the subject of winning prizes came up for review, Shorty surprised Melanie by challenging Colt to a duel at the shooting arcade. She hadn't thought the old guy had it in him to be so playful. "I'll bet I can win a bigger stuffed animal," Shorty said. "The biggest one they got."

"No way." The younger cowboy accepted the challenge. "My name isn't Colt for nothing, you know. I'm a better shot than you anyday, old man."

Shorty narrowed his eyes dramatically. "We'll see about that, boy."

Melanie decided they both resembled characters from the West. Colt had that long-haired, dangerous half-Indian outlaw appeal and Shorty, aside from his sheriff-style mustache, reminded her of the town undertaker, tall, thin and solemn faced.

The twin boys picked up on the macho vibe and started boasting between themselves about which one of them was a better shot, prompting little Joey to puff up his chest and chime in. Sandy and Sarah listened to all the masculine self-glorification, then demanded in a very female fashion just how many stuffed animals they expected.

Colt looked over at Melanie. "I suppose you want a prize, too."

"A big yellow teddy bear for the nursery," she said.

He offered a flirtatious wink that set her heart aflame.

"You got it Mo—" Colt paused but recovered quickly. "Melanie."

She smiled and pretended not to catch his slip. Colt had almost referred to her as *Mom,* something expectant fathers probably did regularly with their pregnant wives. Her heart sprouted wings and silently soared.

Four hours later Joey slept in Shorty's arms, the boys whined because they wanted to stay longer, and the girls had their tiny arms filled with toys from the shooting arcade.

Melanie walked beside Colt, a big pink teddy bear cradled on one shoulder and a blue one on the other. There weren't any yellow bears available so Colt and Shorty decided they had to win one of each "baby" color, so as not play favorites.

Colt chuckled as they headed out to his utility vehicle. "For as much money as we spent trying to win those," he said, referring to the stuffed bears, "we could have bought the little papoose ten more."

She cuddled the fluffy toys. "That wouldn't have been half as much fun."

"I suppose not." He grinned and glanced over at the children. "It was fun, wasn't it? Being around the kids."

"Yes, it was. Almost like being part of a big family."

He chuckled again. "How does becoming a full-time surrogate sound? I might want to do this a second time." He maneuvered his hand around one of the bears and poked her ribs playfully. "Maybe even a third."

Colt flinched, stiffened his neck and blinked rapidly. The paintbrush coming toward his eyes looked dangerous. How in the hell had he become involved in this, anyway?

"Colt, you're going to have to sit still and relax," Melanie said, placing the menacing little brush beside the tray of water colors. She had told him the paint was actually a form of makeup produced in Germany, nontoxic and quick drying.

Now that he'd had time to contemplate the odd circumstances surrounding the body-paint design, he couldn't help but wonder about it. "Did you set me up?" he asked.

"What are you talking about?" Melanie fixed her hands on slim hips.

She looked kind of wild. Sexy. Her paint-splattered Levi's

hugged her legs like a well-worn, comfortable glove and her unbound breasts teased an equally faded T-shirt. Good God, the woman's nipples were as ripe as cherries; they poked erotically against the pale blue cotton fabric. And that fire-streaked hair. A knot at the top of her head loosely secured part of the silky stuff, and the rest fluttered around her face and shoulders, making her look like a modern Gibson Girl, innocent yet seductive.

"This whole thing," he answered finally, trying not to focus on her nipples. "I'm not a model."

She rolled her baby blues. "You think Tiffany and I discussed it ahead of time and deliberately coerced you?"

With a shake of her head and a loud huff, she dipped the paintbrush into a thick cleaning solution that came out of a tube, then wiped it off. Colt watched her, then looked around. Melanie had done a nice job converting the bedroom into a studio. Bright and pleasant, it was furnished with several portable white cabinets, a slanted table and a tall easel. The walls were lined with what he assumed was her work, sketches and paintings, some simple, others elaborate. The entire cabin had been uniquely enhanced by her artistic touch. The rough furnishings in the living room were softened by vintage gypsy shawls and decorative pillows. Scented candles flickered above the stone hearth. Baskets of dried corn had been sprinkled with potpourri and sea shells.

"You're off the hook," she said.

"What?"

Melanie closed the metal paint trays. "Tiffany's in Italy, but I can call her and tell her you changed your mind. I'm sure she'll want me to contact Drake Stallion's agent. Of course, that means I'll have to go back to California for the painting sessions."

Drake *Stallion?* What kind of stupid name was that? "Who's Drake?"

"The exotic dancer," she said. "He's the only logical choice. With Tiffany being out of the country it would be impossible for us to get together to select another model. We both liked Drake, so…"

She intended to fly to California and spend time alone with a guy who takes his clothes off for a living? Suddenly Colt remembered why he had agreed to be The Bandit.

Melanie backed away and Colt found himself staring down at her glossy pink toenails. The expression "barefoot and pregnant" popped into mind. It was still too early to confirm whether or not she'd conceived, but odds were in their favor. She was young and healthy and he had a potent sperm count. Colt narrowed his eyes. No damn way was she flying off to California to paint some stripper's half-naked, muscle-bound body while she carried his child. Drake, the cad, probably had a potent sperm count, too.

"I didn't say I'd changed my mind," Colt said finally, wondering why having a baby with her was making him so damn possessive.

"You accused me of setting you up. What possible reason would I have for doing that?"

Good question. He probably sounded conceited for suggesting such a thing, but he was far from vain and honestly didn't understand why he had been considered for a modeling job. "It's in my nature to be suspicious. My ex did a number on me, remember?"

Melanie squinted at him. "All right then, you're forgiven." She grabbed a paintbrush and nibbled the wood. "But you have to promise to sit still, Colt. No matter what."

"Fine. Whatever." Anything to keep her away from a guy who called himself Drake *Stallion*. "Lets get on with it."

She reopened the paint tin, dampened the brush, dipped it into the concentrated black circle, then studied him. As soon as she tested the consistency of the makeup and brought the brush near his eyes, he jerked.

"Colt!"

"Sorry. I feel like you're going to poke me in the eye." He envisioned himself living out the rest of his life wearing a pirate-type eye patch. One meant to conceal his upcoming blindness.

"I will if you keep jumping around."

"Is it really necessary to paint the mask on, can't you strap one around my head. Like the Lone Ranger?"

"The Lone Ranger?" Melanie laughed. "That's kind of silly."

And a bandit in body paint wasn't? "That's what you said The Bandit was going to wear originally. A cloth mask." Like the Lone Ranger, he added mentally.

She put the end of the brush into the corner of her mouth again. Habit, Colt noticed. Kind of a sexy one. She nibbled on it while she talked. "That's before I was inspired by your heritage. Native American men in tribal paint is strong and sensual. A cloth mask seems hokey now, too comic bookish."

He tightened his shoulders, bit the inside of his lip and clenched his fists. "Go ahead."

"I can't." She set the paintbrush down and removed the headband she'd placed in his hair earlier, sending the long mass falling forward. "Not with you sitting there looking like you've been sentenced to death. I'm just going to have to get you to relax."

She moved closer and began playing with his hair, running her fingers through it. Since he was seated and she leaned over in front of him, her pert little nipples were face level. All he'd have to do was lift her blouse, lower his mouth and...

Oh, God. Now her fingertips were all over his face, tingling and teasing his flesh lightly. "Do you feel better?" she asked.

Unable to speak, he nodded. *Better* wouldn't have been his word choice. *Aroused* was more like it. Her delicate hands glided over his features as though she were molding them, toning masculine muscles and carving angular bones. When her fingers skimmed his lips, she sculpted a pleasured smile.

Melanie smelled faintly of peaches, like fresh-baked pie topped with a frothy spoonful of whipped cream—sweet, succulent and mouthwatering. He realized it was probably lotion because he'd seen peach-scented body products in her bathroom but his imagination went crazy, anyway. He envisioned tasting her skin while she showered, licking every moist, flavorful drop.

As his fantasy engulfed him, she moved to stand behind him and placed her hands on his bare shoulders. "Just a little massage," she whispered.

She had strong, capable hands. Artist's hands. Creative and

agile. Colt heard himself moan, a low sound of submission. He rolled his shoulders and arched his back, giving her free rein. She took it and slid her hands right down the front of his chest to his nipples.

"Damn!" Colt bucked. "Maybe you'd better stop." His urgently aroused tone contradicted his words. He couldn't help it. Every time she circled his nipples, an electrical current, white and hot, shot through his veins.

She removed her hands and he cursed his big mouth. He hadn't been struck by sexual lightning since he was a randy teenager. In his mind, sex with Melanie was forbidden. Just like the good girls from his past. And like the bad boy he still was, he wanted what he couldn't have.

She came forward to stand before him again, and their gazes met and held. "I'm not ready to stop," she said, surprising him. "It's important for me to be familiar with the contour of your body before I paint it."

How could he argue the point? He didn't know the first thing about art, and what harm was there in indulging in a little carnal fantasy once in a while? Melanie would never know. "Oh, sure. That makes sense."

His permission made her bolder. She pushed his legs open and stood between them, then decided his chair needed adjusting. He complied by twisting the knob and raising the chair to her specification.

"Perfect," she said.

Colt's legs were still wide open so she scooted in close. The height of his chair appeared to put him exactly where she wanted him, his naked chest easily accessible.

She started at the base of his throat then moved over his collarbone and down and around his pectoral muscles. Just as she had done with his face, she stroked his chest as though creating it. "You're so hard," she said, "and smooth."

Colt swallowed. She had no idea just how hard he was.

Melanie's deft touch continued. "So strong and virile..." She teased his rib cage and he flinched and broke out in goose bumps. "And ticklish."

When her exploring hands slipped lower, Colt shifted his hips, wondering just how far down she planned to go. The turgid bulge in his jeans would be damn hard to miss. What would Melanie think? This was just art to her.

Colt stole a quick glance at the woman feeding his desire. Art, hell. Melanie was enjoying this as much as he was. Her eyes looked dreamy and a soft smile touched her lips like a secret kiss.

Colt wanted to make love to Melanie. Desperately. But he couldn't. What logical reason would he have for suggesting it, aside from blatant desire? She was probably already pregnant. Sex with her now would prod them into an emotional relationship. Something he clearly wasn't ready for.

As she skimmed his stomach playfully, the muscles contracted and jumped. And when she traced the whorl of hair below his navel, his next breath lodged before rushing out like a strong gust of wind.

She bumped his erection and he nearly flew off the chair. "Ooops." She grinned at him, eyes wide and filled with phony innocence. "Guess it's time to paint."

Eight

"See?" Melanie held a round mirror in front of his face.

Colt stared at his reflection. The painted ebony mask made the white of his eyes brighter and the irises even darker, giving him a sinister appeal. And with his hair parted down the middle and falling to his shoulders, he mimicked a warrior prepared for battle.

"I don't look like me," he said, startled how something so slight could create such a strong physical transformation.

She took the mirror away. "We're not done yet."

"I know." He watched her mix colors on a pallet and test their consistency on her own hand. "The psychedelic part is coming, right?"

Still engrossed in mixing paint, she barely glanced up and nodded. Colt spied the sketches on her worktable and assumed they were renderings of the projected design. It looked complicated and time consuming. Of course, Tiffany was paying for his time. But since he didn't need the money, he planned on adding it to Melanie's charity fund. Through Colt's accountant, she had arranged her surrogate mother's income be distributed among several worthy charities. The first one she had decided on was an organization that aided missing and exploited children. "To bring them home and keep them safe," she had told Colt. "So fathers like you won't lose their daughters."

Her second choice had been to support children from poverty-stricken families in the United States and abroad. Now Melanie had her own brood of foster children. Photographs of innocent, hungry little faces arrived daily, along with handwritten letters, adolescent artwork and grateful parental thank-yous. Melanie Richards was an incredible woman. She answered every correspondence, posted the photos and drawings on her refrigerator and spoke proudly of each child's endeavor.

Colt had moments of weakness when he mourned her participation in his unborn baby's life. Occasionally he found himself imagining the little one suckling her breast or sleeping in her arms. He even wondered if he would have urges to call her when his child took its first step or spoke its first word. Somehow Melanie had become his dearest friend, someone with whom he enjoyed sharing life's joys.

Colt had never been friends with a woman before, which left him often confused and frustrated by his desire to be near Melanie. After all he'd been through, he didn't trust the female gender and kept wondering if she wouldn't end up deceiving him in some way. Sometimes she seemed too good to be true.

"Ready?"

Her voice jarred him back to the task at hand. Modeling. "Yeah, sure."

Neither seemed to have anything more to say after that, so they remained silent for a long while. Colt did his best to sit still as a swirling pattern appeared down the front of his body. Fascinated by Melanie's unusual talent, he watched until a colorful daisy popped up in a disturbing place.

The muscles in his legs jerked. "You're painting a flower around my nipple!"

She barely glanced up. "Uh-huh. Now quit fidgeting."

"Good God, woman, how am I ever going to live this down?"

She brought her face next to his. "No one's going to find out, remember?"

He strove to bore his masked eyes into hers, hoping to intimidate her. "They sure as hell better not." His ranch hands would laugh their butts off, not to mention his team penning partners and the other horse breeders in the county. "I'll look like a sissy."

Melanie burst into laughter. "Colt Raintree, it would take a lot more than painted flowers to make you look like a sissy. You have the body of a god."

A god? Like Adonis? Or maybe the son of a god, like Hercules? He glanced down at the sprouting daisy. Yeah, right. "You're just saying that to shut me up. You name one god who wore flowers on his nipples."

Melanie looked far too amused by the destruction of his masculinity. Her cute little smile annoyed the hell out of him.

"I'm not changing the design," she said, biting back another fit of laughter. "Tiffany's already approved it. In fact, she loved it."

That nut-case would, Colt thought. He raised a black brow wickedly, hoping it made his masked eyes that much more sinister. "Then I ought to be able to paint flowers on yours."

Her smart-aleck smile faded. "What?"

He jutted his chin toward the stimulated bumps under her T-shirt. The woman could have at least had the good sense to wear a bra on the day she defaced a man's naked chest. "You know, yours."

Her entire face flamed. "Colt!"

Laughter vibrated his chest, quirking the daisy. "Humiliating thought, isn't it?"

She crossed her arms over her T-shirt in a self-conscious gesture, and Colt grinned. For a free-spirited California artist, Melanie embarrassed easily.

"I suppose I can alter the pattern a little," she said. "Lose a few flowers here and there."

"A few?"

She narrowed her eyes. "All right. All of them. But that

means I'll have to work out another design. And then I'll have to fax Tiffany with some preliminary sketches.''

"Fine. I'll just go jump in the shower while—''

Her hand flew to his chest. "Oh, no, you don't. You sit right there and be quiet.''

For reasons unknown, Colt did as he was told and she turned away, paced the room, circled him a few times then stood and stared at his naked chest for what seemed like hours. All he could think about was rinsing the stupid daisy off.

"That's it!'' she squealed suddenly.

He startled. "What?''

"The art work on The Bandit was supposed to look like a tattoo.''

He wasn't following her. "So?''

"So think about it. A rugged body like yours is crying out for something primitive.''

All he heard was the faint rumbling of hunger. He hadn't eaten dinner yet. "Huh?''

She splayed her hands across his chest. "A tribal tattoo. You know, bold lines and geometric patterns, native symbols. Something a seventies warrior might wear. A renegade bandit.''

Where did this girl come up with this stuff? "No flowers?''

She laughed. "Not a one.''

"Good. Can I use your shower now?'' He wasn't about to go strolling across the ranch to his house. Not until he scrubbed off every last bit of paint. Covering it with a shirt was too risky. Regardless of the sunshine, with his luck lightning would strike and he'd get knocked unconscious. Of course, then the paramedics would arrive, tear open his shirt to administer CPR and there he'd be—six one, a hundred and ninety pounds with a daisy on his chest.

"Colt.'' Melanie smirked as though she'd just read his mind. "You're welcome to use my shower but the only soap I have—''

"Smells like peaches, right?''

She nodded and he tossed his hands in the air. This woman would be the death of his masculinity yet.

The following week Melanie stood outside Colt's home. He had given her his house key but she couldn't bring herself to use it. Not tonight. Willing herself not to cry, she raised a shaky hand to the heavy door knocker and thumped it against the wood.

A few agonizing moments later, he opened the door. "Hey, what are doing out there in the dark? Come on in."

As soon as she entered the woodsy pine warmth of his home, her throat constricted. Colt looked content. Chest and feet bare, a pair of dark blue sweats fastened low on his hips, he smiled easily. Lately, his moods were light and the time they spent together enjoyable. But not for long. She was about to shatter it all.

"Want some?" He held out a bowl of ice cream.

Unable to find her voice, she shook her head.

"Rocky road," he persisted, lifting the spoon from the chocolate mound. "Guaranteed to cure that long face of yours."

The tears she struggled to conceal surfaced. "Ice cream won't help, Colt."

He discarded the bowl by sliding it onto a nearby end table. "Hey, darlin'…" He swept her hair away from her forehead and collected her tears with the pad of his thumb. "What's wrong?"

Melanie drew a deep breath, cursing the torment that would come with her words. "I'm not pregnant," she said brokenly. "It didn't happen."

The hand against her cheek twitched, then dropped. "Are you sure?"

Her nod was tight. "My…um…you know…time of month came…"

Suddenly Colt looked as ill as she felt. No longer an expectant father, the luster in his eyes turned to a vacant stare. "I guess that's indisputable. No need to take a test or anything."

"No…no need." The home pregnancy kit remained unopened beneath her bathroom cabinet. Two days ago, she and Colt had nibbled from each other's breakfast platters at Mable's before ducking into the local pharmacy like doe-eyed teenagers. One would have thought they were buying their first package of condoms rather than a pregnancy test. Shy, nervous smiles and contained excitement had been exchanged as they read the back of each box carefully.

That same afternoon Colt had pestered her to take the test but she thought it best to wait three or four more days, thinking it might be too early for an accurate result. Her monthly hadn't arrived, but it wasn't actually late yet, either.

Melanie walked over to the sofa and sat down, concerned her legs wouldn't hold her much longer. A sharp pain stabbed her chest as she watched Colt slump onto a leather recliner. Their baby didn't exist. Her womb was empty.

"What if I'm barren?" The question came out before she could stop it. If she couldn't have a child, she'd lose Colt. And if she lost Colt, she'd cease to exist. Her soul would leave her body and she'd float through a colorless world. The tall man with the slow, dangerous smile would be a heart-breaking memory. Sunshine and wildflowers would be no more.

He looked up from his own anguish. "Melanie, don't say things like that."

"You know it's my fault," she said, hugging herself through shuddering breaths. "You've already had a child. The problem has to be with me."

"Problem?" He slid out of the chair and sat down beside her. "The only problem is you're not seventeen and we didn't fog up the back seat of a Chevy."

Another hard breath racked her shoulders. "What's that supposed to mean?"

He managed a smile. "People who want babies don't conceive as easily as those who shouldn't have them do. One time only makes a girl pregnant when she's a teenager. Believe me, I know."

His attempt to cheer her up failed. It only reminded her of the pain she'd felt thirteen years ago when he had married another girl. A pregnant one. "So what do we do now?"

He grinned sheepishly. "Fog up the back seat of a Chevy?"

He was getting closer to easing her pain. She almost smiled through another small flood of tears. "Does that work for people our age?"

"I don't know." His grin faded and his shoulders fell. "I wish you wouldn't cry."

Granting that wish wasn't possible. Her tears had a mind of their own. She wasn't sobbing or making hysterical female noises but she was crying, softly, painfully, each silent tear spilling from her heart.

Melanie reached for the tissues she had stuffed into her shirt pocket. "I'm sorry. I can't help it." How could she tell him her empty womb made her feel inadequate, less of a woman?

Colt stared up at the ceiling. Melanie sensed his discomfort but didn't have the emotional strength to restore it. Clearly her tears disturbed him, yet he seemed reluctant to do what she knew his valiant nature deemed. Hold her, rock her tears away, protect and gentle her, allow her to draw from his strength.

Why wouldn't he comfort her? Had she become less of a woman in his eyes, too? Would he prefer another surrogate? One who had conceived children before?

Melanie looked away and her blurry vision focused on the bowl he had placed on a nearby table. "Your ice cream is melting," she said, unable to bear the morose hush. If he wanted to sever their contract, then why didn't he just say so? Why allow her to sit here in tears while he studied the wood beams as though words of wisdom were etched on their surface?

He lowered his gaze and turned to look at the ice cream bowl. "I'll rinse it out later."

Scintillating conversation, she thought, pain and anger tightening her chest. Damn him for not caring, for not holding her, or kissing her tear-stained cheeks. She wiped her eyes. "I'm going home."

His jaw turned hard, and the taut skin across his cheekbones stretched even tighter. "Back to California?"

Pride kept her from breaking down into racking sobs. Home. She had meant the cabin. "If that's what you want."

A sad softness crept into his voice. "I thought maybe that's what you wanted, that going through another month with me might not appeal to you. I know how much the insemination bothered you. And if we try again, it would mean more inseminations per cycle. Two or three, possibly more. And even then, it may not take. Nature is hard to figure.''

Melanie's heart somersaulted. He had been worrying that she had changed her mind. ''I said I'd stick by you, Colt, and I meant it.''

What sounded like a sigh of relief rushed out his lungs. ''I'm sorry that you have to go through it all over again. Creating life shouldn't be an uncomfortable experience.''

Melanie blinked. Her swollen eyes had ceased their watery torrent. ''I'll survive my humiliation.'' There wasn't a woman alive who didn't dread a gynecological exam, and artificial insemination was just more of the same. Conceiving Colt's child was all that mattered.

A comical, lopsided grin appeared on his lips. ''Just so you know, I was thoroughly humiliated that day, too. I realize I'm a grown man but when I had to turn my sample over to the nurse, I felt like a naughty fourteen-year-old. Hell, I think I even blushed.''

Laughter erupted in both their chests. ''I guess we'll just have to survive our mortification together,'' she said, not at all shocked by his personal admission. Colt's candid personality made him special. The man was open and honest—traits, unfortunately, she couldn't quite claim.

When the laughter faded and the rustic interior of the room absorbed their silence once again, they studied each other. Intently.

As his slow, methodical gaze moved over her hair, down to her shoulders and beyond, Melanie wondered what he saw. Tear-stained cheeks? Red-rimmed eyes? Auburn hair mussed by the night air? And what of her blouse? Why had he fixed his gaze upon it? she wondered, wishing she had worn something prettier.

She gave up trying to read his mind and assimilated his beauty instead. Like an aesthetic reminder of his wayward father, his glossy black mane had been combed away from his face and rested between his shoulder blades in a tight ponytail. Colt had inherited more than Toby Raintree's wild nature. The burnished copper tone of his skin, the slight slant of his eyes and angular cut of his cheekbones were gifts from the man who had charmed his teenage mother. Although evidence of Colt's Native American heritage was strong, the Anglo in him was visible, too. The line of his nose, small cleft in his chin and dark beard stubble peppering his jaw boasted of European ancestry. Of course his smooth hairless chest belonged to that of a warrior, as did long, powerful limbs and well-defined, work-roughened hands.

"Melanie?" Colt's enticing drawl broke through the quiet. "You're attracted to me, aren't you? You know, sexually?"

This time his candor startled her, and she steadied herself as a result. Her brain dizzied as a wave of vertigo took hold. Why would he ask such a thing? Especially now? She struggled to meet his unwavering gaze as the answer slipped out in a near whisper. "Yes. Very much."

"I'm attracted to you, too," he said. "I think you're incredibly beautiful."

Melanie's smile quivered. "Thank you."

Even though deep down she knew he found her desirable, she hadn't expected him to mention it so casually. Fear of rejection kept her from pressing her lips to his and letting him know the extent of her attraction. What if his next statement was a lecture on how improper it would be for them to act on their feelings?

He scooted away, and her heart fell to the floor. Here it comes, she thought. The lecture. *You're my surrogate, Melanie, and it wouldn't be right for us to behave in an unprofessional manner. In the future, we shouldn't kiss or encourage our attraction to manifest itself—*

She lifted her chin and waited for his verbal punch. It came, but not as expected.

"I think we should consider making love," he said, each word edged with a rough timbre. "Going through another insemination doesn't make sense. We both want to touch each other and if we don't follow through, the need will only get stronger." He riveted her with a fathomless gaze. "Would you be willing to make a baby the way God intended?"

Every pore in her body imagined him seeping into it. "Yes."

"I'm not suggesting a relationship. This isn't a vow."

"I understand." Melanie believed just the opposite. The joining of flesh would fuse their hearts, wouldn't it?

"We'll be together until you conceive and after that—" Colt waved his hand in the air as though dismissing something, or someone "—no more sex. Does that work for you, being temporary lovers?"

No, but she wasn't about to say so. Falling in love worked for her, raising their baby together, making love for the rest of their lives. "Of course it does," she said, trying to sound as casual as he. "I'm a modern woman." *Who wants a traditional marriage.*

He smiled. "Good. So it's settled then."

"Sure...but...um..." Suddenly timid, she glanced down at her nails, at the pale-pink polish. Never in a million years could she have imagined a conversation such as this. "How...I mean...when exactly should we first get together?"

Colt had a ready answer, but he looked down at his hands, too. "Next month, when the time is right for you to conceive. Except instead of scheduling an insemination, we'll...ah, plan a date...so to speak."

"Oh...okay."

Her response was followed by a long stretch of silence while they both studied their own hands, the shape of their nails, shade of their skin, length of their fingers. Melanie couldn't remember ever feeling bliss and overwhelming shyness at the same time. It was an odd blend of emotion.

Colt's bare feet hit the floor. "I guess I'll go dump that ice cream in the sink."

Melanie took that as her cue to leave. "Okay...well, I should go. I have some work to do and it's getting late."

He paused, ice cream bowl in hand. "No more tears, right?"

She neared the front door. "No, I'm fine now."

"Yeah." A sexy smile slashed across his face. "Me, too."

Nine

The summer weeks that followed were still blessed with a marigold sun and a vivid sky, but Melanie hardly noticed her surroundings. Today, she strode across the ranch looking for Colt. She had purpose to see him and needed to get it done before her limbs turned to mush or her heart succumbed to panic. One of Colt's young ranch hands had told her he was in the "serving area," whatever that was. She assumed she was headed in the right direction because the youth had jutted his chin toward the chicken coop.

As she passed the empty coops and proceeded on, the serving area and its function became plain as day. She had noticed this fenced area many times and had assumed it was a corral of some kind. It wasn't. Not really.

Blinded by shock, embarrassment and even curiosity, she stopped a short distance away and watched the activity. Shorty and another ranch hand appeared to be assisting a stallion mount a mare. The dark-skinned ranch hand held the mare's head while Shorty, standing near the stud, held the upper portion of the stallion's front leg. Both horses appeared to be wearing bridles, and the massively muscled stallion had its neck extended and upper lip curled as it nibbled gently on the mare's neck.

Melanie decided to slip away quietly and pretend she hadn't witnessed this, especially today of all days, when Colt, who had been observing the mating from the fence rail, turned suddenly in her direction.

He nodded and strode toward her before she had the chance to turn tail and run. "Hey, Melanie." He smiled casually and reached out to touch her hair, something he did often. The familiar gesture sent goose bumps racing down her arms.

She averted her eyes from the scene before them. "Hi."

"Impressive, isn't he?" Colt asked.

She looked up again, assuming Colt referred to the stallion. Thank goodness Shorty's body shielded the part of the stud engaged in servicing the mare. That was something she'd prefer not to be viewing with Colt standing beside her.

Melanie nodded, recalling the name of Colt's prized stallion. "Outlaw's Fancy, right?"

"That's him," Colt responded proudly as he watched the sorrel's performance.

Melanie hoped her cheeks didn't look as hot as they felt. Blushing would make her seem like a greenhorn city girl. Colt's ranch was a breeding-and-training facility. What did she expect?

"Does he fancy himself an outlaw?" she asked. Maybe joking around would take her mind off the situation at hand and what it reminded her of.

"Naw." Colt leaned in close, his breath tickling the side of her neck. "He fancies himself a lover."

The goose bumps reappeared. "That's his job, right?"

Colt chuckled. "Yeah, I get paid and he gets to have all the fun."

They gazed at each other after a silent moment, and Melanie was certain she was blushing. Colt moved even closer and started telling her things she preferred not to hear. By the time he finished talking, she had knowledge of a mare's reproductive cycle, how she was prepared for service, what she did to accept the stallion's advances, how he approached and mounted, the ways in which a mare could injure him, why assistance was necessary and what procedures were done after the mating had taken place.

"So it will be about thirty days before you know if the service was successful?" Melanie asked. In truth, Colt's clinical explanation had eased the awkwardness of the situation and made her realize how common an occurrence this was to him.

He nodded and guided her toward the barn. Even though she didn't look back, she knew the mating had ended and the stallion was being led away. "Of course, Outlaw's not my only stud, but he's always been my personal favorite. He produces some flashy offspring."

Melanie knew Outlaw had quite a reputation in the show ring, too. She had seen the impressive display of ribbons and trophies associated with the stallion. She was also curious as to whether Colt bred mares through artificial insemination, but decided this wasn't the time to ask. Their own experience with that procedure had caused discomfort and heartache, and today she had other news. Good news, albeit it closely related to what she had just witnessed.

She followed Colt to the cluttered office located near the tack room. He opened a small refrigerator and held out a can of grape soda. "Want one?"

"Sure." She flipped the top and sipped slowly while Colt guzzled his.

Melanie knew the paneled room with its pine desk and matching chairs was an addition to the barn. Colt's grandfather had used the sitting room in the lodge for conducting business, but the nature of business at Bluff Creek Ranch had changed. Colt's home was no longer a lodge.

As he shuffled some papers, Melanie sat in one of the straight back chairs and tried to compose herself. Just as she prepared to give him her news, the phone on his desk rang.

He excused himself and answered it. "Hello? Oh, hey, how are you doing?"

Melanie stared at her perspiring palms while Colt continued his conversation.

"Sure, I'll be there. You're doing all right, aren't you?"

She couldn't help but wonder who was on the line. It sounded more personal than business.

"Good. Do you need a ride? No? All right, I'll see you at seven, then. Take care. Bye."

He replaced the phone on its cradle and looked up.

Melanie clasped her hands and eyed her soda can. "So, you have plans later?" Apparently he was meeting someone at seven. It wasn't her nature to pry but tonight concerned her.

"Yeah. Sort of. I attend meetings on Wednesday nights."

"You do?" Strange she had never realized that. But then, they didn't spend every waking moment together. "Meetings, huh?"

He looked her straight in the eye. "AA. I've been going for years."

"Oh, of course." Alcoholics Anonymous. On Wednesdays. Tonight. She knew he was still involved in the program but didn't understand why. He had told her he wasn't the least bit tempted by the desire to drink. And she believed him, wholeheartedly. "I don't suppose you ever miss?"

"No, well, I did when we were in California." He squinted. "What's going on with you, Melanie? You're acting kind of strange."

She reached for the soda, then replaced it without drinking. She glanced at her trembling hands, realizing the impossibility of nibbling a nail. She'd cured that nervous habit by wearing acrylic tips. If ever she wanted her own fingernails back, it was now. "I'm acting strange?"

"Yeah." Colt raked his hand through his hair. "Did that make you uncomfortable or something?"

"What? The phone call?"

"I was talking about Outlaw servicing the mare."

Funny he should mention that. "No, well…sort of, at first. But then after you explained…anyway, that's not really… um…" She hadn't been this tongue-tied in front of him since her teenage years. "It's my…I mean…" She swiped the soda, wet her mouth with a small sip and rushed the words out. "It's time, Colt."

He leaned forward, frowning as though perplexed. "Time for what, darlin'?"

Good God, did she have to spell it out to the man? After Outlaw's performance, she assumed he'd get the picture. Melanie raised her voice a pitch. "You know, *time*."

"Oh!" He widened his eyes, then slapped his forehead. "For you and me."

Melanie twisted the gold chain around her neck. "Yes." She intended to leave the date planning to him.

Colt went on to chastise himself. "God, I can't believe I didn't think of that. I mean, hell, I've thought about it, imagined it almost every day, and then when you finally tell me…"

She swallowed. He imagined what almost every day? Lovemaking, or her telling him?

He stopped ranting and gazed over at her, his dark eyes alight with a feverish sort of glow. Without a doubt the answer to her question was in that sensual stare.

Lovemaking. He'd been fantasizing about being with her. For weeks. Almost every day. Her skin tingled at the thought. He wanted her as much as she craved him.

"I promised Mike, the guy on the phone, that I'd be at the meeting tonight," he said regretfully. "I'm his sponsor, so I don't want to let him down. He's new in the program and having a bit of a rough time."

That was it. Colt remained in the program to act as a sponsor, help others through their struggle. She couldn't help but admire him for that. Maybe if someone had been there for her mother, things would have turned out differently.

He searched her gaze. "I'll be back by nine. Is that too late for dinner?"

Dinner? "No, that's fine."

"I can pick up some Chinese food and come by your place, or would you rather go out?"

She smiled. In a sense he actually did mean a date. Apparently, Colt wanted her to feel like his lady tonight rather than the hired surrogate. Nothing could have pleased her more. "Chinese tastes better at home. I like to eat out of the cartons."

"Yeah, me, too."

After a bout of silence, Melanie stood to leave. Whenever their conversations ceased, she felt awkward. "I'll see you later."

He seemed reluctant to let her go, at least his sensual gaze did. It was riveted on her cleavage now, and the slight amount exposed appeared to be enough to please him. "Any special food requests?"

"Lemon chicken," she said, darting out the door, in desperate need of fresh air. "And sweet-and-sour anything."

Melanie glanced at her alarm clock. Eight-twenty and she still wasn't dressed. What should a woman wear on a date that would ultimately end in lovemaking?

Her prettiest and most feminine undergarments, she decided, displaying several sets on her bed. She gazed at the selection, fingering each one. The pink bra and panties looked too girlish, the white too virginal. Why advertise her innocence? He'd find out soon enough. Melanie glanced back at the remaining choices—floral prints or basic black. The springy flower ensembles didn't seem sophisticated enough, so she opted for black. Would Colt prefer lace or silk? she wondered, anxiety mounting.

She slipped on the silk panties, then hooked the matching bra. The less fuss the better. Colt was a simple kind of guy who appreciated quality. A woman in silk should please him.

Now she had exactly thirty minutes to decide what to wear over her underwear. Pants were difficult to remove gracefully, she thought, rummaging through her closet. A dress was the answer, without pantyhose. There was nothing more unattractive than a naked woman in pantyhose, and although she owned a garter belt and thigh-high nylons, this wasn't the time for them. Too deliberately sexy. Bare legs were the answer, softened with lotion and bronzed by the sun.

The sleeveless black dress she chose hugged her figure without looking ostentatious. The lines of the garment were smooth and sleek, as elegantly understated as the intimate apparel beneath it. A pair of gold sandals dressed it down just enough for an evening at home. A gold-chain anklet added a trace of sensuality.

Melanie checked her appearance in the full-length oak-framed mirror mounted on the back of the bedroom door. As she studied her reflection, she critiqued each physical detail. Minimal makeup improved a heart-shaped face: lip gloss in lieu of lipstick, apricot blush, earth-toned eye shadows and black mascara. An auburn henna had enriched her loosely styled hair, and the black dress exposed legs that were well shaped, even if too petite for her liking. Breasts that boasted a full B cup accentuated her dress with a hint of cleavage.

She was ready. And oh, so nervous.

As she opened the door and glanced back at the bed, she gasped. Her rejected undies were displayed like a provocative lingerie ad. Imagine if Colt had seen them. This was the bed they were going to share tonight. She gathered up the flimsy articles and shoved them into the top drawer of an antique dresser.

Why had Colt chosen the cabin instead of his house? He could have just as easily invited her to his place. His bed.

Melanie smoothed the crocheted quilt, fluffed each pillow and tried not to dwell on her clammy hands or quickening pulse. What did it matter whose bed it was, so long as it happened? She hoped making love meant falling in love. And once she was certain Colt's feelings mirrored her own, she'd be able to reveal her identity. Then no more guilt. Their relationship would be nourished by love and complete honesty.

She checked the time. Ten minutes to spare. Melanie left the bedroom and seated herself on the couch. She had set the wood dining booth with plates and silverware. The built-in table was located just outside the kitchen and within view of the living room; a berry-scented candle flickered in the center of it. Melanie burned candles fairly often and assumed Colt wouldn't think she'd gone out of her way to create a romantic atmosphere. All the lights were on and there was no soft music. Just a woman in a black dress, clay-colored stoneware and a purple candle.

The front door was open. Melanie needed the fresh air and enjoyed listening to the crickets chirp; she'd heard they were supposed to be lucky.

At precisely nine o'clock, booted footsteps sounded on the

stone walkway. She jumped up just as Colt ducked his head through the doorway. Odd that he wouldn't enter without an invitation, she thought. They both knew where the evening would lead, yet they both reacted almost formally to the sight of each other.

"Come in." She relieved him of one of the brown paper bags in his arms.

"Thanks." He followed her to the dining area. "I thought you liked to eat Chinese food out of the cartons."

Now she wondered if setting the table had been the wrong thing to do. "It's a little hard to share the entrées that way. Plates seemed more appropriate."

"That's fine." He placed the second bag next to the one she had put on the table.

"Do you want tea?" she asked. "The water is already hot, so all I have to do is fill the teapot."

"Sure."

Just as she turned toward the kitchen, she heard her name on his lips. "Melanie?"

She turned back to see him leaning against the table, his trademark smile slow and dangerous.

"You look beautiful." The words were spoken in a rich baritone.

"Thank you." He looked beautiful, too. Thick, shining hair fell to his shoulders and his white Western shirt was accented with an Aztec print. "I like your shirt," she said. "It suits you."

He glanced down at the black and red design. "It reminded me of you. Of that art work you're designing for The Bandit."

Her heart swelled. He couldn't have paid her a nicer compliment. The fact she had influenced his taste was a good sign. "I'm almost done with the new design. I'll show it to you later."

A light glittered in his dark eyes. "Okay."

He started unpacking the paper bags, and she stepped into the kitchen to make the tea. The knowing look in his gaze had made her a little dizzy. Her artwork wouldn't be the only thing she would be showing him tonight. Their forthcoming sexual encounter billowed between them like a sheer cloth, tangible yet transparent. A secret neither dared whisper.

The food cartons were scattered on the tabletop when she returned with the tea. She poured the steaming brew into their cups and placed the floral-painted pot on a cloth napkin.

"You must be hungry," she said, eyeing the amount of food he'd provided.

He laughed and scooted onto the bench seat across from her. "I wasn't sure what sweet-and-sour anything was." He flipped open several cartons and peered inside. "So I got everything sweet-and-sour they had."

Melanie, warmed by his concern to please her, took a small sample of each sweet-and-sour entrée and reached for her fork.

He held up two paper-wrapped packages that obviously contained chopsticks. "Do you know how to use these?"

She took one of the packages and tore it open. "Yes, but I'm not an expert."

He opened the other one and grinned. "That doesn't matter. Just eat with them so I can see how it's done. I've always wanted to learn."

She prayed her hand wouldn't shake. "All right. You hold them kind of like a pencil, but you only move your index finger." She demonstrated and lifted a piece of shrimp from her plate. "The top stick does all the work. See?" The shrimp made it to her mouth without incident. No apparent nervousness.

He gave it a try and missed. The chow mein slipped back onto his plate, and they both laughed. "Maybe I should try something bigger, like you did." He went after a slice of lemon chicken, lost it and tried again, only to have the breaded fowl land on the table. Colt retrieved it quickly with his fingers, then stuffed it in his mouth. "You didn't see that." He teased her with a heart-stopping wink.

She marveled at his boyishness. Colt Raintree had many facets to his personality, and this was the side that attracted children to the otherwise roguish-looking cowboy. Gloria's kids were still singing his praises.

"You're trying to use both sticks. Just move the top one," Melanie said, demonstrating her skill once again. She nibbled another shrimp, then looked up to find him staring.

"Come over here and show me."

She continued swallowing long after the shrimp had slid down her throat. Clearly, he was looking for an excuse to be near her. "I'm not sure if I'm teaching you correctly," she said, slipping onto the bench seat beside him. "But I'll do my best."

She placed her hand over his, and he turned toward her. Their eyes met.

"Like this." Melanie quivered a little as she helped him grasp a chicken slice.

They raised it together. It touched his lips and he bit off a piece, then offered it to her. After she ate what was left, he freed his hand from beneath hers, touched her hair and leaned in close.

His warm breath tickled her ear. "I've had fantasies about your mouth," he whispered, caressing her hair. "About how it would feel against my skin."

His erotic admission sent shivers through her body, tingling areas she dared not acknowledge. When she reciprocated with a voice that sounded too husky to be her own, she heard his breath catch. "I think about you, too, Colt."

"At night, when you're alone?" he asked.

She closed her eyes. Tight. "Yes."

He nibbled her earlobe. "Were you naked when you thought about me, Melanie?"

Every inch of her heated and most likely flushed, but she found herself answering his forbidden question. "Sometimes." He occupied her mind day and night, her body clothed and unclothed.

The raw hunger he evoked frightened her. She had a desperate urge to rip his shirt open and cover his warm flesh with her mouth, scrape it with her teeth. Melanie opened her eyes and stared down at her trembling hands. "You make me feel things…want to do things…"

He lifted her chin with his index finger, beckoning her to meet his gaze. "What things?"

Her eyelids fluttered. "I can't…"

"I've embarrassed you."

She struggled to keep eye contact. "A little." A lot. She had never engaged in sensual secrets or even imagined disclosing carnal fantasies to a man.

He placed his hands over hers, and she knew he tried to ease her nervousness.

"How can you be so sexy, yet so innocent?"

What a loaded question. How could she tell him that she had learned to look like an enchantress without actually being one? That she wanted men to notice her, but shied away from their advances? That deep down, Melanie was still Gertrude.

Melanie nibbled her bottom lip. She didn't know how to tell him about her virginity without telling him she'd been saving herself for the right man. An admission like that might make Colt think twice. Now wasn't the time to confess. She would just have to deal with some sort of explanation after they made love.

Melanie glanced over at the scattered white cartons, choosing to avoid the subject of her sexual innocence. "The food's probably cold."

"I'm not all that hungry, are you?"

She scooted out of the seat and began closing cartons. "Not really." Not for food, anyway. Knowing what came next had her torn between excitement and fear. As unsettling as her virginity was, she wanted him. Desperately.

Colt appeared to notice her quaking hands. "I'll help."

They put the leftovers in the refrigerator, rinsed and stacked the dishes then wiped the table. As she emptied the teapot, Colt came up behind her, swept her hair away from her neck and whispered in her ear, "Melanie, I think we need to talk."

She set the teapot in the sink and turned to face him. He looked troubled. "Is something wrong?"

He searched her gaze. "Wrong? Not really, no. It's just that you seem so shy about this. About you and me."

She wasn't sure how to respond so she just stared at him, nibbling her bottom lip again—a habit that had replaced nail biting.

He touched her cheek as if to offer comfort. "I want to do right by you, make tonight special, but—"

"But what?" Was he backing away? Had he changed his mind?

"It's just that I don't want to embarrass you or make you

uncomfortable, but I don't know if I'll be able to stop myself from saying the things I feel. I've never been this sexually attracted to someone before." He expelled a heavy breath. "Good God, woman, I fantasize about you. Want you so bad, I ache."

Melanie's heartbeat tripled. "Then touch me," she whispered, moving into his arms. "Take what you need. Say and feel what you want. Make me yours."

Ten

He led her to the living room, to the Navaho rug in front of the stone hearth, then stepped back to gaze at her. "I want to undress you with my eyes first. And whenever you come through the front door, I want you to remember this moment, this room and us being in it."

She shivered, not from a chill but from warmth. She had never felt so much a woman before, and no man had ever admired her to such an emotional degree. Colt's gaze was sparked with more than just passion. He wasn't just undressing her with his eyes. His soul was involved. She could feel it.

Colt stood, riveted to the floor, his voice vibrating with barely controlled hunger. "So many times I've imagined how you would look without your clothes. How you would feel." A small smile tilted his lips. "Taste."

Melanie drew a deep breath. "I've thought the same thing about you." Her gaze swept over him, at the strength of his jaw, the river of black satin flowing over his shoulders, the way his jeans hugged his masculinity. "I've wondered how your hair would feel when it touched me."

He moved closer. "Where, Melanie? When it touched you where?"

She steadied herself and pushed away the wave of shyness threatening to inhibit her. The concept of foreplay, of touching and teasing was common knowledge, but stimulation through words had never occurred to her. Yet her body had reacted to his confession, just as his had to hers. The permission she had given him to speak freely was a prelude to something wondrous.

Melanie raised her hands to her dress and brushed her fingers across her distended nipples. "Here," she whispered. "When it touched me here."

He came toward her and stopped when they were but inches apart. The air between them appeared to be steaming, heat rising from their bodies.

"What do you have on under your dress?" he asked. "What did you wear for me?"

The fact that he knew she had chosen undergarments with his pleasure in mind caused another shiver. "Black silk."

"Oh, God." A groan rose from his throat. "What does it feel like to have silk against your body?"

Her response was immediate. "The way I've imagined your hair would feel."

That appeared to be his undoing. Without warning, he grabbed her, then crushed his mouth against hers. As her heart thudded in a thick, aroused beat, his tongue drew her into a seduction so powerful she trembled. He was as thirst-quenching as raindrops on a summer day, as clean as freshly fallen snow. He was the earth, the sky and the stars. Everything vital to her. Everything beautiful.

They fused greedily, pressed their bodies close and shifted their hips. He bent his knees and she raised on her toes, both desperately trying to feel the other's heat, make it part of their own.

He ended the kiss only to bury his face in her hair. "I want to take you like this," he said, the words as grinding as the rhythm of his hips. "And I will, but not tonight."

She understood what he meant. There would be another time, a frantic union when he would free himself, push her dress up and tear away the hindrance of an undergarment. But tonight, he would make love to her, as slowly and carefully as he could endure.

She held him close and stroked his back, allowing him time to rein in his appetite, steady eager hands and a rapid pulse. Finally he raised his head and touched her cheek. "Can I undress you?"

She nodded and swallowed.

He reached around and found the zipper on her dress. "I just want to touch you. We won't make love until we're in your bed."

As he opened the zipper and slid the black garment from her shoulders, she fixed her gaze on his hair, on the luster, the midnight sheen. Though she wanted to capture it and let it flow through her fingers, she remained still. This was his moment to explore, to undress her, not just with his eyes, but with his hands. His capable, work-roughened hands.

When the dress pooled at her feet, he touched, just as he said he would. "So beautiful," he marveled, slipping his fingers inside her bra. "And so responsive."

A moment later the silk bra was deftly unhooked and Melanie felt it being removed. Colt leaned forward and kissed one nipple, then the other before flicking a playful tongue across them. And then, as though catering to her fantasy, he buried his face in her cleavage and caressed her with the length of his hair.

Melanie seized his scalp. If the sighs filling the room were hers, she didn't notice; she was much too captivated by the feathery strokes of his hair and the liquid sensation rushing through her veins.

When his mouth covered one nipple and drew on it as would a nursing babe, her womb reacted and the purpose for their loving flooded her with maternal joy. But the suckling was only a sample, a quick tease of what was yet to come. Colt raised his head and lowered his hands to the silk panties and caressed the fabric before pulling them down over her hips. After Melanie discarded them, she kicked her sandals away. Aside from the gold anklet, she was bare. Naked just for him.

He took her hands and placed them against his chest, silently asking her to disrobe him. The Western-style shirt had snaps, so she delighted in pulling it open with one swift motion. But before she could proceed further, he removed his boots and sent them hurtling toward the fireplace.

Melanie waited for him to resume his stance, kissed each flat brown nipple, then grazed his bronzed flesh with her teeth. Tight, corded stomach muscles jumped as she slid her fingers over them, pursuing the thin line of black hair disappearing into the waistband of his jeans. She traced it lovingly with a fingernail, scratching just enough to provoke primitive sounds from Colt.

As soon as she unbuttoned his jeans, he sprang forward, thick and fully aroused. She didn't even stop to think that he wasn't wearing briefs or even boxers; his masculine strength took her breath away.

Like mirror images, they reached for each other and held tight, luxuriating in human warmth and sensual need.

"I want to kiss you here," he said, sliding his hand down between her thighs. "Will you let me taste you?"

Unable to deny his erotic plea, she nodded, and Colt dropped to his knees. The first tender kiss tickled, the second teased and the third swept her into an inferno of desire. The tip of his tongue flicked out like a fiery dart before delving deeply. He sipped and laved the bud of her femininity, kissing the tender flesh as skillfully as he had her mouth. Tentatively, she touched the top of his head, feeling compelled, yet apprehensive to participate.

He slid his mouth to her thigh, nibbled the skin, then looked up, dark eyes blazing. "Do you want more?" he asked thickly.

Melanie thought to look away but didn't. Instead she held his gaze, willing herself to accept the craving his loving had evoked. "Yes."

"Then don't be shy about showing me."

It was difficult not to feel shy about something so intimate, but she realized how much she wanted to succumb to the passion, to be completely immersed. When Melanie reached down to touch his mouth, explore the source of pleasure, he nipped her finger then suckled it, urging her aggression.

As she pushed her hands through his hair and found herself aroused by her own actions, by the need to press herself against him and demand more, he drove her toward the edge. Helpless to Colt's ministrations, she closed her eyes. Ripples of excitement rapidly accelerated to a whirling crest. When the climactic peak finally ripped through her body, she grasped handfuls of his hair and held tight as wave after shuddering wave rocked her.

The sensation of being pulled to the floor ended with her sitting on Colt's lap, her knees bent on either side of him, his mouth covering hers. They kissed and kissed, then kissed some more until finally separating for air.

They stared at each other and smiled. Melanie put her head against his shoulder and he caressed her back. *I love you,* she wanted to say. *With every fiber of my being, I love you.*

"Colt?"

"Hmm?"

She dropped her hand between their bodies and stroked his erection. "Take me to bed."

The sheets were dusky pink, her skin a golden tan, eyes an enticing shade of blue. Colt couldn't remember ever seeing a woman so soft and full of color, so passionate yet so innocent.

The intent of their union was procreation, but somewhere in the recesses of his mind he feared she had bewitched him. Braced above her, he admired her beauty, filling his flaring nostrils with her scent. Peach and woman. Honey and cream. Human salt and sex.

She looked up at him and he wondered how long he could hold off. Desire roared through his blood and pounded in his ears, yet he wanted to absorb her essence before he buried himself in it. The glow from a pale amber lamp highlighted the fiery streaks in her hair and bathed the coral tips of her breasts in warmth. As he flicked his tongue over one cresting tip, she arched and sighed; he knew he was lost.

An image of his child tasting her milk and suckling her sweetness threatened his senses. Although the romantic notion was one he dared not dwell upon, he couldn't stop the words that spilled from him. "Will you nurse my baby, Melanie?"

She stroked his hair and drew his head closer. "Yes."

A hunger like no other engulfed him. Colt closed his mouth over her and feasted, rolled his tongue and tasted and suckled and listened to her soft cry of pleasure. As he stirred against her leg, he rubbed her slender limb like a lusty youth struggling for relief.

She responded in kind, rubbing back at him, holding his head to her breast and encouraging him to sate his appetite. He raised his head and feasted on her other nipple, then rolled it gently between his teeth.

Unable to control his desire a moment longer, Colt tore his mouth away and rose above her. Melanie shifted her hips and parted her thighs, but when he entered her with an urgent thrust, her painful gasp stunned his senses, stilling him.

She stared up at him, her blue eyes wide. Innocent.

A virgin.

Colt swallowed. Good God. He'd just rammed into her without the slightest care. He should have picked up on the signs. No wonder she'd been so nervous.

"I'm sorry, I didn't know...I—"

"Shhh." She pressed her finger against his lips. "Just love me, Colt. I want to feel you move inside me."

He kissed her gently then rocked his hips in a slow yet erotic motion, giving her body time to adjust to his. He watched her, studied her expression, waited for the discomfort etched on her features to fade.

When she smiled at him with a smile so pure, so genuine, he knew it was an offering. She had given herself to him. Her body and, God forbid, maybe even part of her soul.

Lord help him, for the first time ever, he was making love. Not having sex, but making love. Making a baby, preparing through every satisfying stroke to fill her with his seed.

Together they increased the tempo, just enough to crave each other's mouths, to match tongue thrusts with hip thrusts. To scratch and claw and revel in wicked splendor—in the eroticism of fantasy, the pleasure of reality.

Her legs, lean and strong, gripped him as her hands, slender and delicate, traced his jaw, the line of his nose, the indentations below his cheekbones, the arch of each dark eyebrow. "I'm memorizing you with my fingers.'' She raised her hips, taking him deeper. "And my body.''

"Yes." He kissed her fingers, suckling each one. "Remember me." *When our lives are no longer entwined. When you're gone and I'm missing you.*

Unable to endure the agonizing, glorious rhythm a moment longer, Colt felt himself slipping, deeper, into her, into the pressure building in his loins.

"Melanie," he chanted, arching his back and rearing his head. "Sweet...sweet Melanie..."

He wanted to look down at her when it happened, but he couldn't. Locked in the throes of passion, tremors claimed him. Somewhere through it all, through the blinding haze of his release, he felt Melanie shudder, heard her call his name in a voice that took his breath away.

He collapsed in her arms and she held him, stroked his back and absorbed his sweat-slicked skin with hers. Moments later, he forced himself to lift his head. "I'm not too heavy, am I?" She felt tiny and fragile beneath his bulk.

"No, you feel good."

Melanie kissed his shoulder, and he realized she wanted more from him. She wanted the tender aftermath that should come with what they had just shared. Something he'd never given a woman. Not even his wife. Colt had the tendency to roll away from his partner, sleep or zip himself into his jeans and walk away.

That's what he'd do, eventually. Walk away after she gave him a child. But for now, he'd oblige. Because deep down he wanted to give her a piece of himself. She was his friend, his precious, beautiful, female friend.

Colt shifted his weight so he was only half covering her. A sudden rush of guilt raced through him. He'd always wanted a good girl, yet never believed he deserved one. A part of him felt as though he'd tainted her somehow. He hadn't lived a particularly moral life, and neither had his former lovers.

He tucked a strand of her hair behind her ear and pondered their situation. He had taken her virginity, and in nine months, he'd take her child, too. He had nothing to offer her, nothing to give, yet there she was, locked in his embrace.

"It shouldn't have happened like this. Not your first time."

A frown furrowed her brow. "What do you mean, like this?"

"You should have been with a man who's important to you. You wouldn't have waited so long if something like that didn't matter."

She expelled a deep sigh. "Colt, I'm a grown woman."

He gazed down at the lush curves beneath him. "Yeah, I can see that."

"I knew what I was doing. And you are important to me. You're going to be the father of my baby." She skimmed her fingers across his jaw. "This was perfect for my first time. I wouldn't change a thing."

He didn't like that she'd called the child hers, but he decided to let it pass, certain she hadn't meant it in a literal sense. Besides, he had asked her to nurse the child, at least for the first few weeks of its life.

Colt smoothed his hand over her tummy. "Do you think it happened? Because in case it didn't, we should try again."

Melanie grinned. "Right now?"

He couldn't help but laugh. "Sorry, sweetheart, but I need a little recovery time." He could barely wiggle his toes, let alone the vital parts. "You know what sounds good right now?" he asked, not giving her time to answer. "Leftovers. Sweet and sour everything."

"Great idea." She poked his rib. "You go get it and I'll wait here."

"Me? You're the woman."

"And you just ravished me. I need my rest."

"Ravished you?" He laughed again. "Darlin,' I made love to you. When I ravish you, and I promise I will, you'll know it."

She nibbled his shoulder, then lapped it. "After a promise like that, I suppose I could serve you dinner in bed."

The delicious stroke of her tongue had almost revived him. Almost. He leaned over. "Dinner in bed? Does that mean I get to baste you with sweet and sour sauce, then lick it off?"

Immediately her suntanned cheeks reddened. "Colt! Don't even think about it." She bounded off the bed with the top sheet wrapped protectively around her. A moment later an oversize pajama top clothed her svelte form.

Her modesty amused him. If he had been the one going to the kitchen, he wouldn't have thought to cover himself. Not after what they had just done. But then, this hadn't been his first time, either. He noticed the bottom sheet bore a small stain, the evidence of her lost virginity, something he had never expected to encounter from one of his lovers.

While she was gone, Colt closed his eyes and tried not to think about how much he would miss her, miss making love to her. Once she conceived, their intimacy would end. Otherwise their friendship would seem like a love affair.

Sharing their bodies for conception had been a risky venture in itself. But he'd suggested it for several reasons. She had come to Montana to be his surrogate. When the insemination had failed, he feared losing her and the baby she had promised. Regardless of her claim, he wasn't convinced that she would have stuck by him if future inseminations proved unsuccessful. But if they made love, he knew she would stay. Melanie, even through all her innocence, had made somewhat blatant sexual advances toward him. And hell, he wanted her so desperately he could barely see straight, or walk comfortably for that matter. The little wench had given him a permanent hard-on.

Colt frowned. Hard-on, hell. She had penetrated his heart, his callous, distrustful heart. Well, it didn't matter, he decided. It wasn't as if he would fall in love. That foolishness wasn't something he was capable of. Besides, Melanie had a thriving career in California, shopped in Beverly Hills, sipped cappuccino in trendy coffee bars and lived in a beachfront condo. How could a cowboy compete with that even if he wanted to?

"Are you all right? You seem sad or mad or something."

Colt glanced up. Melanie had come into the room, balancing a tray littered with leftovers. He ignored her concern. "That looks good."

She placed the wicker tray on the bed and sat down. "I have

to admit that I am hungry. I was too nervous to eat…you know, before…''

He grabbed an egg roll. He understood; she had been anxious about her first time. ''I got too much food, though. We'll never finish it all.''

Melanie picked up a bowl filled with a variety of entrées and poked a fork into it, skewering several mushrooms and a flimsy pea pod. ''Maybe your ranch hands could eat it for lunch tomorrow. There's a lot more in the fridge.''

Colt swallowed the last of the egg roll and went after the bowl Melanie had prepared for him, then replaced it in favor of drawing the sheet across his hips. He might not be modest, but dropping hot food on his lap could prove painful.

She sat on the bed, her legs crossed Indian style, looking like a girl at a slumber party in her big, plaid pajama top. He smiled. Some slumber party. The naked man next to her was craning his neck to see if she remembered to put panties on.

''What are you looking for? Did you drop something?''

He looked up guiltily. ''Huh? Oh…uh…I've got a crook in my neck.'' He'd go on a panty raid after their midnight snack.

''Do you want me to rub it?''

Colt searched her face for evidence of a double entendre but found none. Lord, she was sweet. He bit his cheeks to keep from laughing. ''Yeah, but not right now.''

''Oh!'' She picked up a fortune cookie. ''Let's see what I got.'' Cookie chunks fell to the bed. ''Here it is—'Your endeavors will succeed.'''

''Sounds promising.'' Colt snagged a cookie off the tray and broke it open. ''Hey! I got the same one.'' He leaned toward her. ''See?''

''I guess this means our endeavors will succeed.''

Colt and Melanie shared a conspiratorial smile. Clearly, their *endeavors* involved making a baby.

His smile remained, even between mouthfuls of food. ''What's your favorite color?'' he asked.

She seemed surprised by the question. ''Why?''

Because she would be the mother of his child, yet he didn't

know the simplest things about her. Colt shrugged. "Just curious."

She propped a pillow against the headboard and leaned back, stretching her shapely, suntanned legs. "Well, that depends."

Colt frowned. He'd just asked her the most generic question possible and she was searching her food for an answer. Melanie confused him at times. "On what?"

She picked up a rib and fingered it carefully. "On whether I'm wearing it, using it as an accent to decorate a house or choosing icing on a cake. Then there's cars, lipstick, and nail polish—"

"Whoa. Time out." He eyed her plaid pajama top, trying to find an easy solution. When his son or daughter asked about its mother, he would have to remember all this stuff. "Start with clothes and go from there."

"Hmm." She followed the line of his eyes and fingered the soft cotton fabric. "It really depends on what kind of clothes—"

"Melanie."

"Okay. Black mostly."

An image of her silk bra and panties came to mind. "Yeah, you look good in black."

"Thanks." She nibbled the sticky rib, licking her fingers as she ate. "That's why I wore a black dress the day we had our first meeting. It always makes me feel a little more self-assured. Sophisticated."

He couldn't resist a chuckle. The woman was sucking sweet-and-sour sauce off her fingers and wearing a pajama top that looked even too big for him. Hardly the picture of sophistication. With that mussed auburn hair and those bright blue eyes, she reminded him of an orphaned kitten cleaning her paws. "What about decorating a house?"

"Well, that depends on where it's located, the style of architecture…" She met his amused gaze and bumped his shoulder with hers. "What's so funny?"

"Nothing. You're just cute, that's all."

"Oh."

She smiled a bit bashfully and once again he found himself intrigued by the innocence of her sensuality. "Go on, Melanie."

"Okay. In ranch-style houses…brown leather and cow prints accented with turquoise. For the beach…white, mauve and aqua. Candy-apple red is my favorite color in sport cars, pale pink in nail polish and natural, sandy tones in lipstick. On a birthday cake I would choose chocolate icing with yellow flowers." She paused for a small breath. "And as far as real flowers go…mixed bouquets."

Colt grinned. If he believed that falling in love was possible, then this woman would be the one he would tumble head over heels for. Of course, he wasn't foolish enough to lose his heart. Not even to Melanie.

"Blue is my favorite color," he offered. "Just plain old blue."

The simplicity of his admission apparently didn't satisfy the artist in her. "No color is plain, Colt. What do you like that's blue?"

He scratched his head, but as he thought about it, he realized she was right. The list that spilled from his mouth sounded almost poetic, even in his cowboy drawl. "A pair of saddle-broke Wranglers, blue ribbons, a slice of fresh blueberry pie," he said with a slight chuckle. "The Montana sky at noon, the Pacific Ocean at midnight…" He turned toward her, the humor in his voice gone. "And your eyes. Your incredible blue eyes."

When Melanie blinked and moistened her lips, Colt placed his bowl on the nightstand and watched her follow suit. As he leaned forward and searched her mouth for everything sweet, pure and seductive she had to give, she caressed his naked chest then slid her hand to his thigh.

The kiss ended with Colt releasing the buttons on the green plaid and straddling her hips. No longer could he tell himself that Melanie Richards hadn't become attached to him, because once he discovered the plain white-cotton panties and the springy curls beneath, Colt saw the warmth in her eyes.

I'm her first lover, he chanted mentally as he tumbled into Heaven in one glorious, earth-shattering motion. *And I always will be.*

Eleven

Noise on every level filled the Carnegie home. The sound of adolescents washing dishes and younger children squealing with laughter could be heard above Colt's and Fred's impersonations of monsters.

The quiet conversation Melanie and Gloria had went virtually unnoticed. The women relaxed on the sagging sofa with steaming cups of coffee after preparing spaghetti, garlic bread and salad for twelve hungry people.

"He looks happy," Gloria said, motioning to Colt, who chased the twin girls around the family room with heavy footsteps and extended arms.

Melanie looked up. Colt had to be the sexiest, most charming Frankenstein monster in existence, and Fred was about the funniest and best-natured Igor a kid could hope for. "Colt adores your children. Every time he sees them, he wants a houseful of his own."

"And just how *is* the baby-making business going?"

Melanie sent her friend a sultry smile. "We haven't missed a day in two weeks."

"Ah-hah. That's why the man looks so content."

"What about me? Do I look happy?"

"You, my dear," the blonde said, leaning close, "are positively glowing. He must be some stud."

"Gloria!"

"Don't you Gloria me. You two couldn't keep your eyes off each other during dinner. It was all Fred and I could do to keep our faces straight. Every time Fred asked Colt a question about the ranch, Colt gazed over at you to see if you were looking his way. Which, of course, you were."

Melanie grinned. "Guilty as charged," she said. "All I can think about is kissing him, then tearing his clothes off."

"I'd say the feeling is mutual, only—" Gloria shook her head in maternal exasperation and nodded to her youngest son, who had pulled Colt's shirt free from his jeans. "Joey's taking care of the clothes part for you."

Calling a halt to the game, Gloria served Neapolitan ice cream in the dining room. Like the rest of the Carnegie furnishings, the oak table showed signs of wear. But as Melanie gazed across the scarred wood, she thought about all the happy Thanksgiving and Christmas dinners that had graced the old tabletop, feeling proud to be considered an aunt to her friend's lively brood.

Joey shoved a spoonful of chocolate ice cream into his mouth. He had traded his scoop of strawberry for the mound of chocolate in his oldest brother's bowl. "We have puppies," he said to Colt. "Real cute ones."

"I know, your dad told me. Queensland Heelers."

"Reds and blues," the boy confirmed with a solemn nod. "They're in the basement so they don't poop all over the house."

"I'm sure Colt could have figured that out for himself." Gloria shook her head when the rest of her children laughed at their brother's remark.

Little Joey's candor reminded Melanie of Colt. They both had the tendency to say whatever came to mind. She imagined Colt had shocked his elderly grandparents a time a two.

"Do you want to take a puppy home for Tall-ee?" Joey asked Colt.

The boy's father adjusted his horn-rimmed glasses. "Tall-ee?"

Colt spoke up. "I think he means Shorty, my foreman. Joey hung out with him at the fair."

The boy whipped his ice cream into a soft pudding when he spotted one of his sisters stirring hers. "He's too tall to be called Shorty."

"Six-four," Colt told Fred. "The old guy's as lean as a fence post and as grumpy as they come, but Joey here handled him just fine."

"Maybe you ought to get the old guy a puppy," Fred offered, apparently anxious to unload the eight-week-old litter. "Queenslands are an excellent working breed."

"Maybe." Colt turned to Melanie. "What do you think, darlin'?"

The affectionate *darlin'* hadn't gone unnoticed by the Carnegies, both parents exchanged a knowing look Melanie hoped Colt hadn't caught. "I think a puppy is a great idea. Shorty needs a new friend."

Joey puffed up his chest, then thumped it with his fist. "Make sure he knows it's from me."

Fred grinned. "Take one with you tonight."

"Maybe even two or three," Gloria chimed in with a smile.

When the older children cleared the table and went into the living room to play a board game, Joey remained with the adults, a serious expression on his freckled face.

"Mom, how come some mommies give their babies away?"

The boy's question jolted every one at the table, but Melanie understood where it had stemmed from. Joey had recently discovered that Trevor, his best friend from preschool, was adopted.

Gloria answered her son patiently, concern wrinkling her forehead. "So other families can have children."

Joey chewed his bottom lip. "Trevor's mom was sad 'cause she couldn't have babies."

"I'm sure she was." Gloria touched her son's cheek. "But the lady who gave her Trevor made her happy."

"Yeah," the child agreed. "All babies need mommies."

Melanie lifted her eyes to Colt. Clearly uncomfortable, he sat stiffly, shoulders rigid, his Adam's apple bobbing. She couldn't help but wonder if he had suddenly realized the importance of a family unit to a small child. Father, mother and siblings.

"How about showing Colt and Melanie the puppies now," Gloria said to her youngest child.

Joey popped out of his seat and grabbed Colt's hand. "Come on."

Colt took the child's hand and reached out to Melanie. The three headed into the kitchen, then through the pantry and down the basement stairs. A grayish-colored puppy barked happily and wagged its bobbed tail as soon as Joey jumped down the last two steps. The boy scooped up the squirming ball of fur and thrust it toward Melanie. "This one's a boy. I call him Sparky."

Sparky sniffed Melanie's hand as she reached forward to scratch his ears. Like the rest of him, the puppy's ears defined unusual breeding: one pointed stiffly toward the ceiling while the other bent comically, giving the dog a lopsided, quizzical look. Melanie noticed Sparky's eyes were as unmatched as his ears, one a rich, warm brown, the other a clear, icy blue.

"He's adorable," she squealed, cupping the furry little face.

Joey handed Sparky over to her. "We got more. See?"

Coming toward them in a variety of speeds and various shades of bluish-grays and orangish-reds were Sparky's siblings. A larger, sleepy-eyed red, which Melanie recognized as the proud but tired mom, padded after the rambunctious litter. The absent father, a muscular blue, patrolled the Carnegies' backyard.

Colt knelt on the basement floor and examined each dog. He held them at eye level, then allowed them to kiss his face with big puppy licks. "They're all fine dogs," he told Joey, "but I think Shorty would like a male. They usually grow up to be bigger."

"Like people," Joey said, eyeing Colt, then Melanie as if assessing the difference in their stature.

Including Sparky, four puppies were males. Melanie kept pushing her favorite under Colt's nose hoping he'd take the hint.

"Are you trying to tell me something?" he asked, on the verge of laughter.

She held Sparky up and waved one of the dog's paws. "He's by far the cutest one."

Colt examined the panting puppy. "His eyes are two different colors. They're not supposed to be like that, you know. And his ears, besides being crooked, are too big for his head."

Melanie felt compelled to defend Sparky's dignity. She remembered how it felt to be less than perfect. "He's unique."

Colt cocked his head and winced at the lopsided little critter. "From an artist's viewpoint, I suppose."

Melanie kissed the top of Sparky's head and the puppy gazed at her lovingly then licked her chin. Colt picked up a husky red male. "We'll take this one for Shorty."

She studied the other dog while cradling Sparky in her arms. The red pup had brown eyes, even ears, and an attractively shaped head. "What about Sparky?" she asked, wanting to throttle Colt. Since when were looks more important than heart or character?

The handsome cowboy grinned. "Sparky is being adopted by us."

"Us?"

"Yeah, darlin', you and me. I figure we can share him." He glanced over at Joey, then leaned in close. "That dog is about the sorriest-looking creature I've ever seen. But for some strange reason I like him as much as you do."

An hour later Colt and Melanie were on their way home. Instead of heading into the garage, Colt had driven the Suburban around the back of his property and parked it beneath a tall, gnarled tree, far from the main house, cabins or barn.

"What's going on?" she asked

"I thought we could sit under the stars a while."

He hopped out and lowered the tailgate, padding it with a blanket. Melanie followed him, puppies in hand. Sparky and the red Joey had named Rudy sniffed the blanket while arranging it to their liking. Both chose the same corner, curled up together in a tight ball and closed their eyes.

Melanie smiled at the puppies then at Colt. "You want to talk, right?"

"Yeah." Colt's sigh blended into the sounds of the night,

with the soft rustle of leaves and quiet buzz of nocturnal insects. "I've been thinking about what Joey said. About all babies needing a mother."

Melanie felt as though she teetered on a live wire. Did Colt want reassurance that he would be a capable mother and father, or was he testing the waters, asking more of his surrogate? The wrong response now could create irreparable damage. Melanie wasn't sure if she was pregnant yet.

"The first time we made love, you asked me if I'd nurse the baby. Do you still want me to?"

He nodded. "Sure I do. I've heard that mother's milk is healthier. And, well, I suppose it would lead to a maternal bond, which is basically what I wanted to talk to you about." He breathed deeply and continued, "I should have made this offer sooner, but I guess it took Joey's influence to shake some sense into me."

Melanie's heartbeat quickened. Thank Heaven for little Joey. Now Colt realized the importance of a traditional family. *I should have made this offer sooner?* Melanie sat up a little straighter and studied his profile, the gentle tilt of his lips, warmth in his touch as he placed his hand upon her knee.

Oh, God. Colt was going to profess his love, the love he'd been denying. Her heart pounded against her rib cage. He was going to propose.

"Do you think that you'd like to be a part of the baby's life?" he asked. "We could work out some sort of visitation rights for you. You could come back here every so often, maybe a couple times a year." He turned to look at her. "I don't want you to do something you're not comfortable with, but I get the feeling that you'd like to get to know your baby. And I've been trying to store information about you, things the child might wonder about, but no matter what I would tell the little one, it wouldn't be the same as knowing you."

Disappointment tightened her chest, pinching her heart. She realized this news should have eased her in some way, yet it hadn't. She had been expecting a proposal, a vow of love and commitment. Melanie battled a riot of emotions. Had she misjudged Colt? Been fooling herself that he'd fall in love with her? Would her dream ever happen or would this be his only offer?

"So I would visit a couple of times a year?"

Colt leaned closer. "It was selfish of me to think I could deliberately deprive a child of having a mother."

She had to change this somehow, strengthen their bond, make him realize he needed her, and that their future child deserved more than a twice-a-year mom. "I would love to be part of our baby's life, Colt. And yours, too. You're my best friend and the most incredible lover I've ever had."

"I'm the only lover you've ever had," he said with a low chuckle.

Melanie looked into his moonlit eyes. "And the only one I'll ever want."

The tone in Colt's voice tightened. "Exactly what are you saying?"

Oh, God, don't let me blow this. She lifted her chin and tucked her hair behind her ears, trying to look calmer than she felt. "If we're going to remain friends then I don't see why we can't go on being lovers."

"You don't think it would complicate things?"

"It's not complicating things now. Why would it later?"

Silence stretched between them. As Melanie waited anxiously for Colt's response, the puppies slept peacefully and he stared up at the heavens as if deep in thought.

Finally he turned back toward her and smiled, his teeth flashing in the dark. "If we're going to go from being temporary to occasional lovers, then maybe you should visit more than a few times a year. I'd like to have a more-active sex life than that."

"Me, too." She bumped his shoulder and sent him a smile of her own. She had increased her place in his life, changed his mind just a little. That proved the possibility still existed for him to fall in love with her. She wouldn't lose faith.

He peered into the Suburban. "What do you say we partake in a little activity right now?"

"In the back seat?" she asked, feeling like a naughty teenager. What she would have given thirteen years ago to have rocked a parked car with him.

Colt nodded toward the puppies. "Think there's any chance of us getting our blanket back?"

"I don't know. Might not be worth the risk. They might wake up."

He began unbuttoning his shirt. "Yeah, we'll let 'em sleep."

They didn't undress all the way. He kept his shirt on but left it open, prompting her to do the same. She even left on her bra and denim skirt. The only thing she slipped off were a pair of red lace panties. Colt unzipped his jeans and led her to the back seat where they kissed and groped.

He rubbed her nipples through the bra, then pushed them up and out of the confinement while she slid her hands into his open fly and made him as hard as she was.

Melanie nudged Colt back onto the seat and lowered her head to his lap. As she kissed the tip of him, he groaned.

"I know I'm supposed to be a gentleman and tell you not to do that," he said, running his hands through her hair, his chest rising and falling anxiously, "but damn it…I want you to."

"Then close your eyes and let me love you," she whispered, snaking her tongue out.

She loved him thoroughly, with her hands and her mouth, with tender kisses and sensuous strokes, with a sliding rhythm that had him chanting her name. The newfound power Melanie felt from giving Colt pleasure urged her to take more of him.

"You'd better stop," he growled, fisting her hair.

She slid her mouth up his body, kissing until they were face-to-face. "Why?"

The rough chuckle that emitted from his throat sounded broken. "Why do you think?"

Rather than answering his question, to which she knew the answer, she asked another one of her own. "Don't you want me to finish what I started?"

He cursed under his breath. "Yes…no. Hell, we're supposed to be making a baby."

Melanie grinned. Colt appeared to be struggling for control. "Are you sure you're ready?" she asked, lifting her skirt just enough to tease him.

He managed what must have been a painful laugh. "Damn it woman, just kiss me and go for a ride. A rough one."

As she impaled herself, they kissed, over and over. *I want him to be mine,* she thought, rocking her hips. *My friend. Lover. Husband.*

Melanie ended the kiss and arched her back. Their gazes locked and they clasped hands. His release was violent and swift. Hers followed moments later as she rode the wave just as he'd requested. Hard, fast and rough.

Thoroughly replete, she hugged him close and rested against his chest.

After an extended period of heavy breathing, he rasped, "The windows are fogged."

She looked up. "Is that good?"

"Uh-huh."

Melanie rubbed her cheek against his chest and listened to the erratic beat of his heart. She assumed Colt's daughter had been conceived in the back seat of a car. He seemed convinced making love in vehicles aided conception.

As Melanie adjusted the position of her face, she caught sight of Sparky and Rudy. "Oh, my God, the dogs are waking up."

Colt lifted his head languorously. "So?"

"So, I don't want them to see me like this."

He squinted. "Like what?"

"This!" She motioned to her rumpled, unbuttoned clothing. "I must look like a harlot."

He laughed and reached out to flick one of her nipples.

She slapped his hand away while frantically trying to right her appearance. Her skirt rode up past her hips and her breasts spilled out of her bra like two perky, oversize oranges. And Colt...

"Zip your pants," she ordered, wondering if he could. His virility was still quite evident.

Sparky and Rudy whined just as Colt fastened his jeans and Melanie secured the last button on her blouse. She swept the puppies into her arms. "Boy, that was close."

He laughed again. "I don't think it's possible to corrupt the morals of a dog."

"Well, you never know." Although Rudy had closed his eyes, Sparky appeared to be studying the humans rather curiously.

Colt exaggerated his drawl. "Yeah, we better be careful what we say and do around the young'uns there. Gotta raise 'em right."

She shifted the dogs, freeing her hand so she could pinch Colt's arm. Apparently he found her naiveté amusing. "So I overreacted a little. I'm not accustomed to being caught in the back seat with some wild cowboy."

He grinned. "I wouldn't worry about it too much. I'm sure the puppies still have the utmost respect for you. I know I do."

Autumn had arrived and with it, golden leaves and cooler temperatures. Melanie slipped on a leather jacket, shoved her feet into Western boots and rushed out of the cabin into the brisk almost-morning air. Three in the morning was an ungodly hour to drop in on someone, but she had to see Colt. Although Colt hadn't asked her to share his home, she felt certain he would welcome her at any hour. Especially tonight.

Sparky chased her, nipping at the silver heel guards on her boots. She swatted him playfully. "You're supposed to do that to cattle, not people."

He barked in response, a high-pitched baby bark that made her laugh. She imagined they were quite a sight: the sleep-deprived, anxious woman, carrying a flashlight almost as big as her equally anxious, crooked-eared dog.

She found Colt's door unlocked. Odd but not entirely unusual. There were occasions when he neglected to lock his door, a living-in-the-country habit most Californians wouldn't comprehend. Of course, Melanie wasn't like most Californians; she still carried Montana in her soul.

Sparky darted past her and raced down the hall, skidding as he turned into Colt's room. She had intended to wake Colt with a kiss, but now Sparky would beat her to it. As Melanie entered the rustic bedroom, the puppy greeted her beside a vacant, unmade bed.

"Where's Daddy?" she asked the dog. The master bathroom was empty, as well.

Melanie searched the house and discovered Colt was nowhere to be seen. Where would he go at this hour? Ranch life started at the crack of dawn, but the sun had yet to rise.

"You'd better stay here," she told Sparky. First she planned on checking to see if Colt's truck was in the garage, and if it was, then she'd look for him in the barn. It was possible one of the horses had taken ill, and if that was the case, Sparky would be underfoot.

Since the Suburban was in the garage, Melanie walked carefully across the ranch, guiding her direct path with the oversize flashlight. The ranch had security light fixtures, but she wasn't taking any chances. As soon as she neared the barn, the white glow spilling from beneath the door told her Colt was probably there. Someone had turned the lights on.

She entered the building and followed male voices to a box stall near the rear of the building. Melanie stood quietly and peered into the enclosure. Colt knelt in a bed of straw, holding a mare's head in his lap, soothing it with gentle strokes and soft words. Shorty was there, too, and Melanie realized the men were assisting the mare with delivering a foal. By the animal's exhausted appearance and the sweat beading across Colt's brow, she assumed the labor had been unusually long and difficult.

She heard Shorty's "That a girl" when two front legs appeared in the bluish-white plastic bag being expelled from the mare.

That's the baby, Melanie thought, raising a hand to her own stomach. She watched the miracle of birth, tears lining her eyes as the foal broke through the water bag. An adorable damp little head could be seen along with the forelimbs.

Immediately, Shorty removed the membrane obstructing the baby's nostrils and allowed the delivery to continue. The mare's position had changed now as she sat up to look at her foal.

By the time the new mother examined her baby, Colt noticed Melanie. He came toward her with an exhausted but happy smile.

"Hi," she whispered, watching the mare enjoy her role as a parent.

He leaned across the stall opening and kissed her cheek. "We were worried there for a while, but everything turned out fine." Colt looked back at the foal. "The little guy'll be on his feet soon."

Melanie studied the gangly foal. Still damp, its ears pasted to its head, she thought it was the most adorable creature she'd ever seen.

Shorty spoke in a low voice. "Go ahead and get yourself some sleep, Colt. I'll keep an eye on things here."

"Thanks," Colt responded just as quietly.

He left the stall and joined Melanie. "Want a cup of hot chocolate?"

She nodded and followed him to his office, where he slipped into the adjoining rest room to wash his hands, then returned and placed a glass pitcher in the microwave. "What brought you out here at this hour?" he asked, shoving some papers aside and seating himself on the edge of his desk.

She smiled, remembering the last conversation they'd had in his office. "You. I went to your house but you weren't there, so I assumed you were in the barn."

The bell on the microwave sounded and Colt hopped up. He removed two coffee cups from an overhead cabinet and sprinkled the powdered chocolate into them, then poured the water and stirred. "You must be feeling pretty frisky to come looking for me in the middle of the night," he said, handing her a cup.

She smiled. Typical male response. He thought she wanted to make love. "Colt, I'm pregnant."

He nearly spilled his steaming drink. "Are you sure?"

Melanie nodded. "I had planned to take the test this morning, but I couldn't sleep, so I figured the result would be the same at 3:00 a.m. as it would be at 7:00 or 8:00. It was a plus sign, a very distinct plus sign."

He threw back his head and let out a high yelp before sweeping her into his arms. "I'm going to be a dad," he exclaimed, a grin splitting from ear to ear.

"And me a mom," Melanie squealed as he spun her in a small circle.

When Colt stopped spinning her, he opened her jacket and slid his hand under her sweatshirt. The masculine hand warmed her stomach.

His dark eyes sparkled. "How many weeks along are you?"

"Five or so, I think."

Colt removed his hand and formed a tiny space between his thumb and index finger. "The baby is about this big, and its heart is already beating."

She smiled and stroked his cheek. "How do you know that?"

He grinned. "Just something I memorized from a book. In three more weeks it will be about an inch long and weigh a gram. And its little facial features will already be shaped, along with elbows, knees, fingers, toes, even buds for the first baby teeth."

Tears misted Melanie's eyes. "That's amazing."

He kissed her. "So are you, Mom."

They held each other and swayed together, luxuriating in life. He rubbed her tummy, and she cradled her head against his broad shoulder, thinking about the tiny being they had created.

I love you, little one, she said mentally. *You and your Daddy.*

Time passed, but neither noticed. They were where they belonged, in each other's arms, celebrating their miracle.

Finally Colt spoke. "Do you want to go back and see the foal? He should be on his feet by now."

"I'd love to."

Melanie decided Colt's horses had become significant in their union. Prior to making love with Colt for the first time, she had witnessed Outlaw serving a mare. And now, on the day she confirmed her pregnancy, a healthy foal was born. A male. A colt.

As they walked to the new mother's stall, Melanie spoke her thoughts out loud. "I think we're going to have a son."

The man next to her stopped. "Why?"

She shrugged. "I don't know, just a feeling."

He grinned and spouted off more of his book knowledge. "At

this point in time, the sex organs haven't formed, but I suppose there's always mother's intuition.''

As they approached the stall, Shorty was exiting. ''Everything's fine,'' he said, smiling at both Colt and Melanie.

She noticed the older cowboy smiled more often and suspected that Rudy, the sturdy little Queensland Heeler pup, was the cause. Shorty had taken to the dog like a dolphin to the sea.

Colt squeezed Melanie's hand. ''We just wanted to check out the little guy.''

The older man nodded, and Colt broke out in a big anxious grin.

Shorty eyed Colt's exuberant smile. ''Something else going on I should know about?''

''I'm going to be a dad again. Melanie just told me she's expecting.''

''Well, that's wonderful, son.'' Shorty extended his hand. ''Congratulations.'' After the men shook hands, Shorty turned to Melanie. ''It's a real nice thing you're doing for Colt. He's been wanting another youngster for quite a while now.''

She smiled. ''Thank you.''

''Melanie's going to take an active role in the baby's life,'' Colt said. ''A child needs a mother.''

As Shorty's gaze locked with hers, Melanie felt as though he had just looked into her soul. Gertrude's soul.

''I'm real glad to hear that,'' he said. ''Congratulations to both of you.''

As the older man tipped his hat and sauntered off, Colt led her closer to the stall and they both gazed at the foal. Standing on long, reasonably steady legs, he digested his first meal.

''He's precious,'' she said softy. ''And his mother looks so proud.''

Neither spoke after that, but Melanie felt certain Colt shared her next thought. In less than eight months, she would be nursing their child.

Twelve

"**C**aught ya!"

Melanie spun around. "Shorty! My God, you scared the death out of me."

The older man laughed, and she realized this was the first time she'd ever heard his raspy laughter.

"You're feeding that mare snacks again."

She grinned sheepishly. "True, but Cinnamon loves me for it."

The horse snorted and nudged Melanie's shoulder. Shorty shook his head in apparent resignation. "How are you feeling?" he asked. "I hear mornings are a might rough."

Melanie offered Cinnamon the rest of the sugar cubes and answered the old cowboy's question with a slight shrug. "Colt insists that I eat breakfast, so he fixes me something every morning. An hour later I throw it up."

Shorty leaned against a stall door and smoothed his mustache. He wore the same dusty tan hat, coarse denim workshirt and pointed brown boots every day, but the smile quirking his bottom lip looked fresh. "That boy never could cook worth a damn."

Melanie met Shorty's amused gaze, and they both burst into a small fit of laughter. Cinnamon bobbed her head and whinnied as though she, too, had tasted Colt's cooking.

"He's driving me a little crazy," she said when their laughter simmered. "But he means well."

"Seeing a woman ailing upsets him a might. He was just a boy when his momma took ill, but he did everything he could to alleviate her suffering." Shorty fingered a halter hanging on the wall beside him. "Colt and his momma were real close."

Melanie pushed her hands into her pockets. "What was she like?"

"She was a nice gal. Pretty and well mannered, a bit shy. When Colt's papa first came to work here, she used to lurk around corners and watch him with those big brown eyes of hers. And when he'd catch her staring at him, he'd wink and she'd pert near faint." Shorty pushed back his hat and scratched his bald head. "Kind of like another little gal I used to know. Only she used to follow Colt around."

Melanie's heartbeat doubled. "And how did Colt react to this girl following him around?"

The older man steadied his gaze. "Same way his pa used to with his ma. He'd smile and wink at her, make her weak in the knees, I suspect."

She swallowed a little nervously, then raised her chin, realizing there was no point in pretending anymore. "How long have you known?"

"Didn't until now, not for certain, anyway. But I started putting two and two together that night at the fair. That starry-eyed look you kept giving him was just too familiar. And then when he'd gaze back at you and wink, well…"

"I'm in love with him."

Shorty nodded solemnly. "I know."

"And I changed my name a long time ago. That had nothing to do with coming here."

"Gertrude is a perfectly nice name," the older man said. "You shouldn't be ashamed of it."

She twisted the lining of her pockets. "I know. I thought it was an okay name, too. My mother named me after her grandmother, and I was always very proud of that. But when the other kids started teasing me about it, I didn't want to be Gertrude anymore."

"So you moved away to California and became Melanie?"

"I was hit by a car a couple years after I moved to California. The reconstructive surgery changed how I looked, so I decided to use my middle name and become someone totally new."

Shorty studied her. "That did confuse me some—that you looked kind of familiar, yet you didn't. But after I figured out who you probably were, I thought you must have just filled out is all. You were a skinny teenager, but you had those big, trusting eyes and a genuine smile. Can't change those things."

He shifted his lanky stance. "Even years after you quit coming to the ranch, Colt still seemed worried about you. 'What do you think ever happened to that sweet girl with the blue eyes?' he used to ask me. 'Do you think she's all right?'"

Melanie gazed up at the barn roof, trying to blink back her tears. Colt had never forgotten her.

The older man leaned forward and lifted a slightly crooked finger to her cheek. "Nothing would please me more than to see you and the boy raise that baby together. But remember, keeping secrets will only come to no good. I don't like talking behind his back like this."

Melanie nibbled her lower lip, her eyes still lined with tears. "I plan to tell Colt the truth, but just not yet. I've been waiting for him to accept the fact that he loves me. I think he's close but not quite there."

"Don't wait too long. Colt has the right to know who you are."

Unnerved by his suggestion, she fidgeted with the buttons on her jacket, then pulled it closed. "I guess I'd better get back to the house. Colt asked me to have lunch with him."

Shorty raised his thin gray brows. "He's not cooking for you, is he?"

"No." Melanie managed a smile. "He had some business in town and said he'd bring back something from the diner."

"All right then, you get along." Shorty shooed her toward the door. "You're eating for two now."

As Melanie stepped into the crisp afternoon air and headed toward the main house, the old man's words echoed in her mind.

Colt has the right to know who you are.

She stopped beside the abandoned chicken coop and expelled a labored breath, hoping to expel her guilt along with it. Not only had she kept her identity from Colt, but she'd pulled Shorty into her secret as well.

But I can't tell him, she thought, certain Colt wasn't ready for the truth. Regardless of what Shorty had said, she knew a premature confession could have a disastrous effect. No, she couldn't chance it.

Melanie passed the arena, willing herself to stay calm. She focused on the familiar sights and sounds, on the crunch of leaves beneath her feet, on the clouds billowing across the sky. But as she stepped onto the stone walkway leading to Colt's house, tears rolled down her cheeks—tears of guilt.

"Oh, no," she whispered, as Colt suddenly appeared from the corner of the house. He must have parked the Suburban on the side of the property and walked around.

Abruptly Melanie turned in the opposite direction. She couldn't meet with Colt looking and feeling the way she did. She had to go to her cabin first, wash her face and dry her eyes.

Praying he hadn't seen her, she darted across the walkway and lost her footing. Instinctively she attempted to brace the fall, skimming her hands and bare knees across the hard surface.

Colt screamed her name. She looked up to see him racing toward her. Within seconds, he was there on the ground with her. "Are you okay? Are you hurt? Oh, God, you're bleeding."

She glanced down at her knees, at the blood seeping through the scrapes. "I'm fine," she said, pressing her stinging hands against her chest. "I guess this wasn't a very good day to wear a dress."

"Are you sure you're all right?" Colt moved his hands over her body as though checking for broken bones. "What happened? Why did you turn away like that? God, you scared me."

He lingered over her tummy. "Your stomach doesn't hurt, does it?"

"I'm fine," she said again, struggling to contain another flood of tears. "And the baby's fine. I'm just a little scratched up, that's all."

Apparently satisfied that her bones were intact, Colt gathered her into his arms and cradled her against him.

Her tears rushed forward.

"Oh, darlin'," don't cry." He rocked her in a slow, soothing motion. "Come on, let's get you inside."

He carried her into his house and deposited her gently onto the sofa. She sat on the cowhide surface and stared up at him while he eyed her rumpled appearance.

"I'll get the first aid kit. Just don't cry anymore, okay?"

Before Melanie could utter a response, he disappeared down the hallway. She removed her jacket, then studied her palms— a little red and swollen, but no blood. Somehow her knees had taken the major impact, and even then, those injuries were minor.

Colt returned with a well-stocked first aid kit. He handed her a box of tissues. She dried her eyes and blew her nose while he sat on the end of the coffee table and tended her knees. After he cleaned and bandaged the scrapes, he touched her cheek. "Do you feel better?"

She nodded. "I'm sorry I scared you."

"Why were you so upset? I could tell something was wrong even before you fell."

"I umm…" She fumbled, the sound of Shorty's voice ringing in her ears. *Colt has the right to know who you are. Keeping secrets will only come to no good.*

Unable to think clearly, she offered the only excuse that came to mind. "Shorty caught me feeding Cinnamon some treats. I guess I felt…umm…I don't know…bad because I promised Shorty I wouldn't spoil Cinnamon anymore."

Colt's eyes came alight with anger. "Did Shorty snap at you again? Damn him—"

"No!" She interrupted in the old man's defense. "He was very nice…he…" *Figured out who I am, told me I should be honest with you.* "My hormones are out of whack. I overreact to everything."

"Yeah, but why were you avoiding me?"

Quickly, a half-truth surfaced. "Because I didn't want you to see me crying over nothing. I just can't seem to control my emotions."

Clearly out of his element, he offered comfort by way of a textbook diagnosis. "Pregnant women are known to be overly emotional in their first trimester. Don't worry about it too much. You should feel better soon."

Anxious to move on, Melanie changed the subject. "Weren't we supposed to be having lunch?"

"Damn." He made a face. "I dropped the food when I tore off after you. I guess we'll have to fix something here."

"I'll do it," she offered, reaching forward to gather the extra large Band-Aid wrappers he'd scattered onto the coffee table. She needed a few minutes alone to catch her breath.

Colt jumped to his feet. "No, I can—" He stopped in mid-sentence and stared at her hands. "What happened to your nails?"

Melanie curled her fingers. Her swollen fingers and chipped nails were a sorrowful sight, but hardly a crisis. "I removed the acrylic tips this morning. I know they look awful, but the last time I went to get them filled, the smell made me sick. I guess it's the pregnancy." She scooped the Band-Aid wrappers into a tidy pile. "Besides, I'm not sure how safe that chemical is. My manicurist wears one of those little masks."

"Your other nails were fake?"

She met his stunned gaze. "A lot of women wear them."

Confused by his reaction and seeking relief from a maelstrom of emotions, Melanie did something she hadn't done in years. She nibbled a fingernail.

Colt felt his body jolt. Déjà vu. He'd heard the expression before, but had never experienced it. Until now. This moment had happened before. Years ago, another little girl had sat on that couch, gazing up at him, biting her nails.

Gertrude. Shy, tiny Gertrude—the girl Melanie reminded him

of. Gertrude had been injured, too. She had fallen from one of the rental horses and sprained her ankle. Colt had carried her into the house and doctored her, just as he'd done with Melanie today. He had never forgotten Gertrude, not her adoring blue eyes or her fragile, broken fingernails.

Colt closed his eyes and swallowed, pushing Gertrude's image away. He didn't want to see her. Not now, not like this.

But a moment later, when he raised his eyelids, she was still there, sitting on his grandparents' cowhide sofa, staring up at him.

"You're her," he said. "Oh, my God, you're her."

The hand against Melanie's lips began to shake. "I…" She sniffed and blinked before a rain of tears spilled down her cheeks.

Colt stood riveted to the floor, feeling as though he'd just been kicked in the gut by the only woman he'd come to trust. "Don't you cry. Don't you dare cry."

He never knew what to say or do when a woman cried. Tears made them seem vulnerable, and he knew she wasn't as vulnerable as she appeared. She had deceived him from the beginning. "You never had any intention of giving up the baby, did you?"

Melanie pulled a wad of tissue from the box and dried her cheeks. "It's not what I wanted, but I told myself I'd go through with it if I had to."

He dragged his hand through his hair. "I don't believe you. If you had planned on giving up the baby, you would have told me who you were. Damn it, you tricked me."

She twisted the damp tissue. She looked young and sweet in her oversize denim dress and bandaged knees. He glanced away, telling himself not to fall for all that innocent femininity. She was no different from his ex-wife.

"I swear, Colt. I never meant to trick you. My intentions were honorable, but you kept stressing how you wanted a professional relationship with your surrogate. If I'd told you I was Gertrude, you wouldn't have hired me." She trapped his gaze. "You knew that I—that Gertrude had feelings for you."

Gertrude had been so sweet and pure. So trusting. But Melanie wasn't her anymore. "So what the hell are you getting at?"

"I'm in love with you, Colt. I've always loved you."

When his heart clenched, he damned her silently. "Love isn't based on a lie, Melanie."

"The only thing I lied about was my identity. I wanted us to make a life together, but if you didn't fall in love with me, I vowed to myself that I'd be noble and give up the baby." She cradled her tummy protectively. "But I couldn't agree to do that now, and I pray you won't ask me to. This baby deserves two full-time parents." Once again, her eyes glistened with tears. "I hadn't been able to anticipate the maternal bond of carrying a child, of waiting for that first flutter of life. I'm a mother now, Colt. In my body and in my heart."

"Yeah, and I'm a man who wanted to be a father again. A man who hired you as his surrogate. I wasn't looking for a wife." And he wasn't buying her story about her original intentions being honorable. It had all been a lie, a deception. "You're nothing like Gertrude used to be."

Her eyes remained open on his, big and blue and full of pain—pain he didn't want to see, didn't want to recognize.

Melanie gave a labored sigh. "You're right. In some ways I'm not her anymore. She was shy and afraid. And she lacked the confidence to tell you how she felt about you." Melanie continued to cradle her tummy. "But Gertrude grew up, Colt. And you helped her get there. You treated her with kindness when she needed it most, and you taught her to believe in herself. Gertrude became Melanie because of you."

Rather than acknowledge her words, Colt studied the changes in her face. Apparently Gertrude had become Melanie because of plastic surgery. Her nose had been shortened, her cheekbones altered, even her chin looked different. And then there was her hair—red instead of brown, and her body, although still tiny, had developed muscle tone and rounded curves.

She'd traded Montana for California, and with it, a lifestyle that appalled him. She should have kept the features she was born with instead of paying some Beverly Hills doctor to play

God. She'd become rich and spoiled—cosmetic surgery and a condo on the beach. How typically Hollywood.

"Was this some kind of game to you, some frivolous challenge? Breeze back into your hometown and fool everyone with your new face?"

She lifted her chin—her fake chin—in what seemed like a gesture of defiance. "No."

"Then why the plastic surgery? Why the big charade?"

She brought her hand to her cheek, touched it as though it didn't quite belong to her. "I didn't have a choice. I was involved in an accident that destroyed my face. My nose was broken and my cheekbones shattered. Everything had to be repaired."

Colt listened while she relived what had to have been a nightmarish ordeal. He tried to block out sympathetic images of her, of little Gertrude, broken and bleeding, young and afraid, all alone and far from home.

Once she stopped talking, she chewed her fingernail again and gazed up at him with those eyes—those familiar blue eyes. Eyes he had recognized, even commented on. "You should have told me who you were that night on the beach, the night I admitted you reminded me of someone else." He plowed his hand through his hair for the second or third time. "You played me for such a fool."

"I wanted to tell you, but it was too soon. I wanted you to love me first."

Love. She wanted him to love her, to give her what he'd never been able to give any woman. "I'll say it again, love isn't based on a lie. That's just not the way it works."

Colt glanced away, his heart throbbing with an unbearable ache. How could he ever love a woman who had purposely deceived him? How could he ever trust her?

"I can't handle this." He backed away. "I've got to get out of here." Spinning on his heel, he shot out the door, leaving Melanie alone on his couch.

She'll cry again, he thought, as a gust of fresh air swept over him. *But only for a while. In a hour or two, she'll fix herself some lunch, nourish the life in her womb.*

In Colt's mind one crucial detail remained undisputed. Melanie wanted their baby as much as he did.

Thirteen

Fifteen days later, Colt paid his dinner bill at Mountain Mabel's. He'd eaten there every night that week and the week before.

Mabel handed him his change and tapped the pencil behind her ear, pushing it into her starched hairdo. "Guess you'll be back tomorrow night, huh?"

"Yeah." No more home cooking. He had barely set eyes on Melanie since he'd discovered her identity, let alone enjoyed one of her meals.

Colt exited the diner and came face-to-face with Melanie in the parking lot. He startled. "What are you doing here?"

"Looking for you."

She dropped her car keys into an oversize purse. The big bag made her appear smaller, as did the loose-fitting jacket and baggy pants. He wondered if her tummy had expanded. He hadn't touched her stomach in over two weeks.

"So you found me. What do you want?"

"For you to be polite, for one thing. You've been rude, Colt. You barely speak to me, and when you do, you're far from civil."

He raised an eyebrow. "So you think approaching me in public is going to make a difference?"

"If that's what it takes. I refuse to be ignored. We have to talk sometime."

She adjusted the bag on her shoulder. It looked heavy, he thought, wondering why women carted around everything they owned. He clenched his fists to keep himself from reaching out to touch her. Her hair had blown across her lips. Lips he longed to taste once again. Lips that had spoken deceitful lies.

Two elderly women walked past. Colt recognized Margaret Sneed, a sales clerk at the pharmacy, and the biggest gossip in town. When she glanced back, he scraped a booted foot against the asphalt.

"If you want to talk, we can sit in the car for a while," he told Melanie, as he returned Margaret's wiggle-fingered wave. "No point in giving the locals an earful."

Melanie followed him to the Suburban. He unlocked the doors, and they settled into the bucket seats. A stream of silence ensued. She studied his profile while he stared out the windshield. The setting sun shot streaks of gold across a scarlet sky. It reminded him of fire, of her hair.

"You wanted to talk, so talk," he said, his tone deliberately impatient.

"I have a doctor's appointment tomorrow."

He whipped his head toward her. "Is everything all right?"

"Fine. It's just a routine visit. Do you want to go?"

He glanced down at her tummy where her hands rested protectively. "Do you want me to?"

She nodded. "I miss you, Colt. I miss sharing leftovers at midnight and sleeping in your arms." Her tongue darted over her lips, moistening them. "I miss feeling your hands on me."

"Don't do this." He turned back to the setting sun, silently cursing its beauty. "I don't want you anymore."

Her voice softened. "Yes, you do."

She was right. He did. Just the nearness of her sent his body into a thunderous arousal. But lust, he told himself, meant nothing. Not as long as his heart remained intact.

She moved closer. "I'm not going away."

He gritted his teeth. Her lotion-scented skin wafted through the vehicle like peaches on a spring day. He could almost taste her. Almost. "We've already decided you're going to be part of our baby's life, but being part of mine is altogether different."

She touched his shoulder briefly, gently. "You'll always be part of mine, Colt. Don't you realize how you've helped me grow? You used to tell me time and time again how sweet and smart I was, until eventually I began to believe you. You nurtured me in that bad-boy way of yours." She gazed at him, laughing softly in fond remembrance. "And every time you winked at me, my legs quivered and my heart skipped a beat. It was all I could do not to melt at your feet."

Her words made him ache, as did the tenderness in her tone. The past and all those bittersweet memories haunted him daily. "I don't want to talk about this."

Melanie crossed her arms. "Fine, Colt. Live in denial, but don't you dare treat me badly in the process." She kicked the floorboard. "Boy, have you changed. You're certainly not acting like the valiant cowboy you once were."

He blew a nervous breath. His emotions, all two thousand of them, were tied up in knots. "Fine. I'll be civil, okay? But that's all."

A smile tilted her lips. "That's a start." She opened the door, looking far too beautiful for her own good. "Bye, Colt. I'll see you later."

He watched as she strode away, marveling at how the sunset played upon her hair. Was his heart still intact? Colt closed his eyes and damned himself. Now he wasn't so sure.

Later that evening Melanie entered Colt's house without an invitation. She made her way to the kitchen and lifted the cover on the peach cobbler she'd brought along. It smelled heavenly, and the cream she'd whipped looked rich and tantalizing. After helping herself to a tall glass of milk, she removed two dessert plates from the cupboard.

Colt's kitchen was spotless, but then he had a housekeeper. Of course, he didn't cook much for himself, either. Unused kitchens managed to stay clean.

"What in the hell are you doing here?" Colt stormed into the room, his hair dripping beads of water onto his bare shoulders.

"I told you I'd see you later."

"I didn't know you meant tonight."

"Well, I did." She sliced a piece of the treat and heaped a spoonful of whipped cream on top.

His nostrils flared. "What's that?"

She thrust the plate at him. "Peach cobbler. Gloria gave me the recipe."

He set his jaw stubbornly. "I don't like peaches."

Melanie rolled her eyes. She knew he loved peaches. He loved the taste and the scent. Her lotion always made him hungry—for the fruit and for her. It wasn't easy living without him, pretending she didn't hurt, that she didn't cry herself to sleep at night.

"Suit yourself." She dipped a spoon into the cobbler, catching a frothy glob of the cream.

Colt watched her like a wary cat, his exotic-shaped eyes darting between the plate and her mouth. He looked gorgeous. His freshly showered skin glowed like polished brass. Pale gray sweatpants, his usual lounging attire, rode low on his hips.

"Maybe I'll try a small piece," he said, scooping a large helping of the cobbler onto the other plate.

He tasted the dessert and moaned. She managed a heavy-hearted smile. Winning his affection back wasn't going to be easy. It would take a lot more than a pan of warm peaches.

Melanie leaned against the tiled countertop. "I thought we could watch a movie tonight."

"No, thanks. I'm turning in early."

"Do you want some company?"

He spilled his next bite. The pastry crumbled back onto his plate. "No."

She sipped her milk and tried to act casual even though her heart pounded like a native drum. "Well, just in case you change your mind—"

"I won't." Colt narrowed his eyes. "Stop trying to seduce me, Melanie."

An ache flooded her chest. What she had in mind went beyond seduction. She loved him, and she believed he loved her. Somewhere deep inside his tortured soul, he loved her. She knew because of how badly he was hurting. At times, she could see her own pain reflected in his eyes. "I wouldn't know how to seduce a man. I'm new at this, remember?"

He shifted his feet uncomfortably. "Can we talk about something else? Something less personal?"

Melanie sighed. Healing his heart might take a lifetime. "Like what?"

He finished his cobbler. "Like how Sparky's obedience training is coming."

She found herself giggling. She'd enrolled Sparky in one of those puppy kindergarten classes, but the Queensland managed to flunk out. "The trainer suggested private sessions. Sparky's just too hyper for group lessons. The other dogs distract him."

Colt set his plate aside and grinned. "That pooch is a pain in the butt."

"True, but he's ours."

The grin faded. "Yeah, ours."

They stood silently then, gazing at each other with pained expressions. The baby was theirs, too. She closed her eyes, opened them. They hadn't discussed her parental rights, or the original document she had signed. "I want to be a full-time mother, Colt. I couldn't possibly just visit a few times a year."

"I know." He pushed his damp hair away from his forehead. "We don't have a surrogate contract anymore. I destroyed it."

A rush of air escaped her lungs. "Thank you," she whispered.

His expression remained tight, his mouth set in a grim line. "I did it for the baby. Regardless of how I feel about what you did to me, I know you'll be a good mother."

Regardless of what you did to me. Those words hurt. No matter how many times she had tried to tell him that her intentions had been honorable, he refused to listen. He just kept saying love wasn't based on a lie.

"I figure we'll share custody," Colt said, interrupting her thoughts. "That's the way it should be."

No. They should be married, raising their child in the same house. She touched her stomach and pictured the tiny being growing there. "We're having a boy," she said. "I'm sure of it."

"A son." Colt's features softened. He stepped forward and reached a hand out. "Do you have a tummy yet?"

Melanie raised her blouse. "A little one."

His hand connected with her skin. She shivered on contact.

Colt smiled and poked her belly button. "Are you sure that's not from the cobbler?"

Her heart lunged forward and chased his smile. "It's the baby."

He rubbed her stomach with circular motions, gently introducing the tiny life inside to its father. But a moment later, he removed his hand and stepped back as though he'd crossed some self-imposed line by touching her, even if it had been to address his child.

"How are you, Melanie? Are you still sick?"

Sick at heart, she wanted to say. "Every morning."

"Are you keeping crackers by the bed?"

She nodded. "Nothing seems to help." And she missed his meddling, his awful scrambled eggs and oddball nausea remedies. He used to offer a new one daily.

Colt sighed, a heavy, masculine sigh. "You were right about being civil toward each other. If you're stressed, the baby will feel it. And more than anything, I want a healthy, happy child."

"Me, too," she said, wishing she could fall into his arms.

Another awkward silence stretched between them. She glanced down at her shoes, willing herself not to cry. If she met his gaze, she would. Tears would spill from the broken pieces of her heart.

"You look tired, Melanie. You should go home. Get some sleep."

She imagined he spoke the truth. Although the pregnancy taxed her, she had been incapable of a deep, relaxed slumber. She woke nightly and reached for him, only to discover emptiness, not just in the bed, but in her soul.

"I'm okay," she said, knowing it was far from the truth. Neither of them was okay, and at the moment, she had no idea how to make things right.

For Colt, the weeks that followed didn't get any easier. Every time he saw Melanie, his heart battled his pride for control. There were too many times, like today, when he worried the ache in his chest might be love.

Colt scrubbed his hand across his face. The land, *his* land, and the mountains surrounding every lush green acre usually soothed him. Today it didn't. Today he felt nothing but that damn ache where his heart thumped much too heavily.

He leaned against a tree and let the rough bark scrape his shirt. Damn it, why couldn't he learn to trust? Melanie claimed she hadn't meant to trick him; she just hadn't anticipated the strength of her maternal feelings. From the beginning she knew the possibility existed that she may have to give up her child— a baby conceived with the man she loved.

Once again Colt's heart knocked aggressively against the ache in his chest. Did she really love him that much? Of course she did. No matter how many times he told himself otherwise, Melanie was still Gertrude—a gentle girl with a pure soul. A girl who wouldn't lie. A girl who had been willing to give up her child to the man she loved—offer him the most precious gift of all.

Melanie. Sweet, perfect, beautiful Melanie. How could he have ever doubted her?

Oh, face it, Raintree, you're in trouble. You're in love, but your pride refuses to accept it. You don't want to admit a woman holds your heart in the palm of her hand.

Colt glanced down at the colorful leaves scattered at his feet and imagined his future child as a toddler, its eyes filled with wonder as it lifted a burnished, gold-tipped leaf. Children found pleasure in the simplest of things. They could play with a cardboard box and squeal with delight, enjoy wrapping paper as much as a gift, pound on a metal pot as though it were actually a drum.

The leaves crunched as he walked over them en route to his house. What he needed was to immerse himself in the nursery, the room where his future child would sleep…the room of past and present magic. Yes, he needed to go there and rock himself in the big padded rocker Melanie had bought, close his eyes and explore his heart.

Colt passed the roping arena with long, anxious strides. He would find solace in the nursery with its polished wood crib and antique cradles. The splendor of the baby's room would grant him the familiarity he needed. Colt had been a father before, but he'd never been in love. The mere thought scared him senseless.

As he walked, an image of the nursery came to mind. Both he and Melanie had added special touches to the room. She had painted the ceiling blue and warmed it with puffs of billowing clouds, offering their baby the sky. And he had chosen two antique cradles, one for the stuffed animals and the other in honor of his ancestors. The second was actually a cradleboard— a baby carrier constructed of a wooden base covered with soft animal skin. Glass beads and long fringe decorated the hide. Colt sighed. Just picturing the cradleboard gave him comfort.

He entered the house and headed down the hall toward the nursery, but stopped when he heard the soft creak of the rocker coming from the partially open door.

A lump formed in Colt's throat. Melanie must have needed to immerse herself in the nursery, too. He remained where he stood, out of sight, but close enough to hear the gentle sound of the rocker. He couldn't walk away. Colt needed to be near her, feel her emotions, remember the quiet confessions she had made, recall her words in his mind.

The only thing I lied about was my identity. I wanted us to make a life together, but if you didn't fall in love with me, I vowed to myself that I'd be noble and give up the baby.

Colt exhaled a ragged sigh. He wished he had the courage to walk into that room and tell Melanie he believed her. Tell her he'd been wrong. So very wrong. But if he did, he'd have to tell her that he loved her, and he didn't know how to say those words out loud.

As the creak of the rocker continued, Colt pictured Melanie secure in the chair, her hands resting on her tummy. She had purchased the oversize rocker so he, too, would fit comfortably in it.

Dear God, what else had she told him? What other words had he ignored?

You used to tell me time and time again how sweet and smart I was. You nurtured me in that bad-boy way of yours. And every time you winked at me, my legs quivered and my heart skipped a beat.

Colt smiled, remembering those silly winks and grins he'd tossed her way. She had been the most fragile girl on earth, and without realizing it, he'd helped her grow into a successful, self-assured woman.

Why hadn't he realized that sooner? He shook his head. Because he'd been acting like an idiot, that's why. He kept accusing her of being deceitful when her only crime was loving a stubborn, deafhearted man.

Melanie, the beautiful artist. The woman who had loved him forever—loved him enough to cradle his babe in her womb—a child they had conceived from a loving, sensual joining. Colt's mind drifted back to the night he'd taken Melanie's virginity, and he shivered, unable to shake the erotic chill that crept up his spine. The memory washed over him like a sexual balm, like cool, feminine hands caressing his skin. Melanie had given him two precious gifts that night—her body and her soul.

They belonged together. He knew that now, just as sure as he knew his own name. Melanie Richards should be his wife—his lifelong partner. They were meant to be a family—two people raising their child in a safe, nurturing environment.

Colt closed his eyes. He could see the three of them on long winter nights, cuddled in front of the fireplace, Christmas lights blinking on a tall evergreen, colorfully wrapped packages piled beneath it. And there would be more children later, he decided, happy, healthy children to run barefoot through the rich dark soil and breathe crisp mountain air.

He opened his eyes, stared down the long, dim hallway. How could he ever propose to Melanie after what he'd put her through? Yet someway, somehow, he would have to. He intended to marry Melanie Richards, be the husband she had always dreamed of.

With his heart stuck in his throat, Colt backed away and left

Melanie alone in the nursery. He took a deep breath, then exited the house. Colt Raintree had some soul-searching to do.

Several hours later Colt stepped onto Shorty's redwood porch. The old cowboy sat in one of the high-back chairs he kept near the front door. The cabin belonged to Colt, but the porch belonged to Shorty. He had made the addition years ago. Colt assumed Shorty had built the porch as his own private window to the earth. The Montana sky above and sculpted mountains beyond offered a breathtaking view.

Shorty looked up but didn't speak.

Colt seated himself in the other weather-beaten chair while Shorty whittled a small piece of wood. It struck Colt as such a grandfather-type thing to do that he decided to keep silent until Shorty acknowledged him. Elders deserved respect, even gruff old cowboys.

They sat quietly for a time, listening to sounds of the earth. Wind rustled the tops of trees as several birds pecked the bark for food. If a man strained his ears, Colt thought, or imagined hard enough, he could hear the peaceful lull of the mountains: fish splashing in streams, pinecones falling to the ground.

Shorty turned to Colt, his agile hands still shaping the wood. "Something on your mind, son?"

"I'm going to ask Melanie to marry me."

"That's real fine. The right thing to do."

"I don't want it to be your average proposal, though. I'm thinking of arranging a surprise wedding."

Shorty's hands, much like his passive expression, didn't falter. "Doesn't sound quite possible. Weddings aren't like birthdays."

"I'll find a way to make it possible. I've got plenty of imagination." And too damn much pride. The idea came to him as an alternative to admitting outright that he'd been wrong. He couldn't just walk up to her and say, "I'm an idiot. Will you marry me?" If he surprised her with secret wedding plans, she'd simply forget he'd been acting like a fool. Besides Melanie loved surprises. And he owed her something special, something uniquely romantic—the gift of all gifts. Immediately his mind soared into overdrive. He'd have to trick her at first, but later, when she learned the truth, she'd fall into his arms. Hold him close. Kiss him. Cry tears of joy. He wouldn't even have to hang his head and apologize. The surprise would be apology enough.

Colt's mind drifted into images of the future: laughter at dawn, family picnics at noon, fairy tales at bedtime. And midnight lovemaking, he thought, under a starry Montana sky.

"Look," he said, hoping to make Shorty understand the importance of his plan. "The only way I'm going to be able to pull this off is if you and the Carnegies help me. I need you to come through on this one, Shorty."

"I'll do what you ask. You and that little gal should have been married months ago."

After Colt left Shorty's cabin, he increased his strides, telling himself not to run. He felt like the vibrant, wild-eyed teenager he had once been. His life, though, had changed, and he'd learned plenty in the process. This time the bad boy of Mountain Bluff intended to marry the right girl—the auburn-haired beauty from California.

Fourteen

In the beginning of her second trimester, Melanie decided dawn was her favorite time of day. No longer a victim of morning sickness, she rose bright and early every day to help Colt work with the new foal. Recently Colt's civil behavior had worked its way back into friendship. She knew he still waged a private war, though. He loved her, but refused to say it. And he wanted her, too. The platonic hugs they shared never failed to quicken his pulse or glaze his eyes. On more than one occasion, he had nuzzled her neck and "accidentally" pressed his chest against her distended nipples. She, in turn, would "accidentally" brush his arousal with an errant hand. Desire played like an erotic game between them, one neither had yet to verbalize.

Melanie turned her attention back to the foal. The youngster had one of those long, registered names, but she called him Bam-Bam because, for a little guy, he was exceptionally strong and prone to stomping his hoofs and rattling the ground.

Instead of participating with Bam-Bam at first, Melanie would observe Colt and how carefully he approached the young animal, gradually earning its trust. She noticed Colt had restrained the feisty foal by cupping one arm around its neck and the other around its rump. He had explained that if you try to restrain a young horse by holding its head, they tend to rear backward.

The next step had been fitting Bam-Bam with a head collar, then teaching him to lead by pushing him from behind. She had also learned how important it was for a foal to get used to having its feet handled, something little Bam-Bam hadn't taken kindly to. It had been during one of these sessions that he had earned his nickname.

"When will he be weaned?" she asked as they secured the foal and its mother in their stable.

Colt removed Bam-Bam's head collar, and the little one nudged the cowboy playfully. "When he's about five months old."

As they walked to Colt's office for their usual hot chocolate break, Melanie tugged on her denim jacket and tried not to think about herself months from now, waddling around in snow. She already missed California's sunny climate.

While sipping the warm brew, she let Colt in on the latest news. "Gloria and Fred are going to renew their wedding vows. Isn't that romantic?"

He sucked a melting marshmallow into his mouth. "Sounds like a waste of time and money to me. They're already married. Why would they want to do it again?"

"Because they're in love," she snapped back, wishing Colt were more like Fred. The anniversary-wedding ceremony had been Fred's idea. The Carnegies' anniversary was later in the season, but they had decided to schedule the ceremony before the snows set in. "Gloria asked me to be her maid of honor."

Colt rolled his eyes. "You mean they're going to go through that baloney all over again? Bridesmaids and all that nonsense?"

She glared at him. "Their kids are really excited about it. The twins, Sandy and Sarah, are going to be flower girls, and Joey will carry the rings. The older girls will be bridesmaids and the other boys ushers. And since Shorty has become like a grandfather to Joey, Gloria asked him to walk her down the aisle."

Colt burst out laughing. "Shorty? Our Shorty?"

Melanie slammed her cup down. "I fail to see what's so funny about Shorty participating in a wedding."

"Sorry." Colt waved his hand in front of his face. "Somehow I just can't picture him in a monkey suit."

She leaned in close and poked his chest with her finger. Colt's flippant attitude about something as sacred as a wedding boiled her blood. "Well, picture yourself in one, mister, because Fred wants you to be his best man."

Colt shook his head. "Tell him thanks but no thanks. I'm not interested in going anywhere near an altar when there's a wedding in progress."

"I can't tell him that." Melanie was at her wit's end. She had hoped this event would inspire Colt to move forward in their relationship, to quit pretending the love between them didn't exist. "You're going to be Fred's best man whether you like it or not. And later this week, we're going shopping with Gloria. I need to pick out a dress and you have to get fitted for a tux. All the other men have already ordered theirs."

"When is this wedding?" he asked with a sour expression.

"In three weeks. It was sort of a last-minute idea. And Shorty, by the way, has been very helpful in planning it. He even suggested your house for the reception."

Sarcasm sharpened Colt's voice. "Well, wasn't that thoughtful of him."

"Yes it was." Melanie lifted her nose in the air. "Shorty's a very generous man."

"Yeah, with somebody else's house," he mumbled.

"I thought it was a wonderful idea. This ranch is a perfect place for a reception. Besides, Fred and Gloria are our best friends. We owe them this."

Colt lifted his legs onto the desktop and folded his arms behind his head, looking too arrogant for his own good. At the moment Melanie wished she wasn't so madly in love with him. The man didn't have a romantic bone in his body.

"What's this *we* stuff?" he asked. "You're talking like you and I are a couple."

She touched the tiny mound in her tummy. "*We* made a baby as I recall. And you're just dying to get me back into bed." A move she knew he was close to making. "I'd say that makes us a couple."

In typical male fashion, he zeroed in on the sex part. "What's lovemaking got to do with this?"

She thrust her shoulders back and tilted her chin. "Nothing, I suppose. After all, you claim we're not a couple. And as a free agent, I think abstinence is best. There's no way I would consider resuming our sexual relationship at this point in time."

His perfectly formed jaw went slack. "What kind of bull is that? For weeks you've been meowing after me like a Siamese in heat."

"A Siamese in—" Melanie had the unholy urge to kick his chair out from under him. "Well, you've done a pretty fair imitation of a tomcat, you know."

"Yeah. So, what's the problem?"

You and your noncommittal attitude. "I just don't think it's appropriate for us to sleep together right now."

"You don't, huh? Well, that's too bad." He dipped his hat and gazed at her through hungry eyes. "Because I planned on visiting you tonight, you know, with some Chinese takeout."

Melanie ignored the all-too-familiar ache in her loins, the sexual pull. Chinese food had become their favorite aphrodisiac. Sweet-and-sour everything. "I'm not interested."

"And just when will you be interested?"

When you admit that you love me, you big lug. She shrugged. "I don't know. I'm too busy to think about it. Coordinating a wedding is a big job." With that said, Melanie stalked out the door, leaving Colt with his mouth agape.

Colt nudged Gloria's shoulder when Melanie took a stack of satin and lace into the fitting room. "Now she refuses to sleep with me," he complained. "But I suppose she already told you that."

Gloria chuckled as she studied a pink dress lined with a stiff, ruffled petticoat. "Mel has a stubborn streak, you know."

"Yeah, but you don't have to look so amused by it." He didn't think being sexually rejected by the woman he intended to marry was the least bit funny, even if he had tricked her into believing he thought weddings were a waste of time. A man's sexual prowess was no joking matter, and Melanie had never shunned his advances before. Damn good thing this wedding surprise was about to unfold. His libido couldn't take much more.

He grabbed the pastel dress out of Gloria's hand. "Pink clashes with Melanie's hair. I want her to wear off-white. Silk with those little pearls sewn on. Something slim fitting. I hate big, puffy dresses."

She snagged the pink lace number back. "I was looking at this for me. And I already told Melanie to choose something in cream."

Cream. Colt liked the sound of that.

They both turned toward the three-way mirror when Melanie came out of the fitting room wearing a long-sleeved, high-necked Victorian-style gown.

Colt wrinkled his nose. "You're all covered up."

She ignored him. "What do you think, Gloria? I could pin my hair up." Melanie swept her hair into a loose knot on top of her head and held it there. Several fiery strands fell about her face.

"It's very ladylike," Gloria said, jumping when Colt pinched her arm. "But it's probably too much dress for someone your size. Try something with less material."

Melanie studied herself then dropped her hands. "I suppose you're right."

When Melanie retreated, a tall, thin woman appeared. "May I help you?" she asked Gloria.

"Yes," Gloria answered, apparently eager to explain the up-coming surprise.

As the saleslady led Gloria through the boutique, Colt went back to the mirror to wait for Melanie. She came out wearing a satin dress trimmed with lace and little rhinestones and glanced around, apparently for Gloria. "Colt, why don't you go for a walk or something?"

Not likely. He had plans for today, and they included the right dress. "You were there when I got fitted for that monkey suit, now I want to see what dress you're going to wear."

"Why?" She ruffled the rhinestoned hem. "You think formal weddings are dumb."

"Yeah, but since I got suckered into this, and I'll be walking down the aisle with the maid of honor, I want to be sure she's not wearing some stupid-looking dress." He lowered his voice. "And let me tell you, there are some ugly gowns in here. Hell, most of them are so big, they look like two women could fit into them."

She gave his denim attire a haughty once-over. "And I suppose *you're* a fashion expert?"

"No. But I know women's bodies, and yours looks better in something smooth and slinky."

Their gazes locked in the mirror, and a soft blush colored her cheeks. Colt recognized the feminine glow. It came over her whenever she was aroused.

"And you should put your hair up, kind of loose and messy, like you did a few minutes ago," he said, moistening his lips.

She stared at his mouth, then flinched as though she'd been caught thinking something immoral. "I'll wear my hair however I feel like it," she snapped back at him, sounding like a bratty teenager.

Angry as she was with him, he still thought she was adorable, even in the rhinestoned dress. Colt grabbed his hair. "I'm thinking of putting mine in a ponytail."

"That's probably a good idea," she said, as though struggling to make polite conversation. "But I like your hair loose, too."

He grinned. "Yeah. You like to run your hands thought it. And you like the way it feels on your—"

"Colt!"

He followed Melanie's sight to see Gloria and the saleslady coming their way.

The clerk displayed four silk dresses on a nearby rack. "Would you like to try any of these, dear?"

Melanie let out a soft, little gasp when she touched one of them. Colt and Gloria exchanged a knowing look. "Try it on, Mel," Gloria coaxed. "It's beautiful."

"Do you think it's appropriate for the maid of honor during a day wedding?" Melanie asked the saleslady.

"The ceremony is at three," Gloria chimed in quickly. "And we can wear whatever we want, Mel. After all, I've decided on pink since it's my best color."

"Your friend is right," the other woman said. "Since this wedding is a renewal of vows, it's not necessary to adhere to tradition. And this dress would look lovely on you."

Melanie grinned and snagged the gown greedily. "I'll be right out."

Moments later, she emerged from the fitting room. A shiver tingled Colt's spine.

The gown, elegant in its simplicity, was stunning against Melanie's honeyed complexion and fire-tinted hair. The silk slid down her lithe form like a river of cream. The sleeves and open neckline were delicately adorned with the tiny pearls Colt had requested.

He smiled his approval, and the sales clerk knelt to adjust the hem line. "It will need some minor alterations," she said to Melanie. "But I think it's absolutely gorgeous on you."

Gloria moved closer. "Me, too."

"It is beautiful," Melanie said, then raised her arm and glanced at the tag. "Oh, my goodness. I can't spend this much on a dress I'll probably never wear again."

Gloria looked over at Colt. Since the Carnegies struggled with a moderate income, Melanie had insisted on paying for her own dress, but neither Colt nor Gloria had thought the extravagant artist would balk at the price of a gown. Colt, of course was footing the entire wedding bill, but Melanie wasn't to be told. At least not yet.

Colt chuckled. "Complaints from a woman who wears ostrich cowboy boots?"

She touched the fabric reverently. "This costs more than my boots. Besides, I honestly don't think this dress is appropriate for the maid of honor. It looks more like a bridal gown."

Colt and Gloria exchanged yet another glance. "I think this is my cue to leave," she told Colt quietly, then turned to Melanie, "I'm going to look around a bit more."

When Gloria and the saleslady disappeared, Colt smiled. He

had planned this moment to unfold just as it had. He wanted Melanie dressed in pearls and silk when he revealed his surprise.

He stepped forward so his reflection shone beside hers in the mirror. "That dress *is* a bridal gown, Melanie. The upcoming wedding isn't Fred and Gloria's renewal of vows."

In the mirror her bright blues eyes lifted to his. "What exactly are you saying, Colt?"

Excited now, he rocked on his heels. "The next shop on my list is a jewelry store. I figured we could pick out the rings together." He smoothed his hair and studied her, anxious to see the tears that would soon glaze her eyes. "I'm asking you to be my wife, Melanie. That is, if you'll have me."

Her eyes didn't tear. And instead of throwing her arms around him, she stood motionless. Was she in shock?

"I'm sorry, Colt, but I can't marry you."

Every ounce of air fled from his lungs as a maelstrom of emotions filled them. She had turned him down. He'd planned this wonderful surprise, and the woman carrying his child had just refused to marry him. The invitations had already been sent, the caterer contacted, flowers ordered. Colt locked his knees to keep them from buckling. He'd been so sure. So damn sure. "But it's what you've wanted from the beginning—"

"No." She shook her head. "What I wanted was for you to fall in love with me. After that, I assumed marriage would be the next logical step. But you see, you've never told me that you love me. I've been waiting and waiting, but you've never said it." She fingered the tiny pearls on the neckline of the dress. "I can't marry a man who won't admit that he loves me."

Colt cursed his stubborn pride—the pride that had kept him from saying what she needed to hear. Apparently a surprise wedding wasn't nearly as romantic as those three simple words. He stepped up behind her, lowered his head near her shoulder and inhaled her soft, feminine scent.

With his heart lodged in his throat, he slipped his hands around her waist, around the tiny mound where their baby slept. "I want you to know you're the first woman I've ever said this to."

She looked up at their reflections in the mirror, and he smiled.

She stood lithe and graceful in her silk dress while he wore a rough texture of denim. But even so, they appeared to fit perfectly together.

Colt pressed his lips to her ear. "I love you, sweet Melanie." He turned to face her. "I love the color of your eyes, and the way your nose wiggles when you laugh. I love the shape of your body and the feel of your hair." He clasped both of her hands and watched her eyes turn watery. "I love the way you lift your chin when you're mad and try to hide your sniffles when you're sad."

He realized he could go on forever and never say it all. "I want to marry you, Ms. Richards, because I love you and I want us to spend the rest of our lives together." He took a deep breath and continued. "And I'm sorry I didn't say it sooner. I should have apologized for the way I treated you before, but at first being in love scared me." He clutched her hands a little tighter. "It doesn't scare me anymore, though. I think loving you feels incredible."

"Okay," she whispered through the tears trailing down her cheeks.

He grinned. "Okay what?"

"Okay, I'll marry you," she said, before she fell bonelessly into his waiting arms.

Melanie stood in the nursery, surrounded by the warmth of native wood and fuzzy toys. She moved toward the antique cradle and smiled. A thick, downy coverlet lay in the interior, a fur as primitive and beautiful as the cradle itself. Colt must have placed it there, knowing it belonged amid the old-fashioned charm. Many a child had slept in the tiny bed. Round, sweet babies from the century before. Babies born to pioneers and ranchers, men and women who had worked the heart of the land.

She looked over at the second cradle, the Cheyenne cradleboard placed carefully upon a small table. It too had sheltered sleeping babes, children with soulful brown eyes and shining black hair. Cradleboards were often made by a family member or friend, then given to the expectant parents as an honored gift. Someone had taken great care to construct this one, she thought.

They had decorated the hide with intricate patterns of tiny glass beads and added long strips of fringe to drain off the rain.

Melanie touched her tummy. Colt's heritage, and hers too, were displayed in this room. And soon she would rock their baby to sleep in the big padded rocker and whisper nursery rhymes and Indian folklore.

"I thought I'd find you here."

She didn't turn to the sound of Colt's voice; instead she waited to experience his approach—the familiar sound of ranch-worn boots, the subtle scent of masculine cologne. Only hours before, they had chosen gold bands to seal their upcoming union. He had insisted on buying her an engagement ring, as well, even though their formal engagement would be short. He'd claimed the diamond would forever remind him of the day she'd accepted his proposal. She smiled as his scent drifted closer. To Melanie, the glittering stone would immortalize the moment Colt Raintree had professed his love.

He encircled her waist, and she leaned into him. As he caressed her tummy, a memory flashed into her mind. They had stood together in the maternity shop in California, her stomach enhanced by a pillow, his hands placed upon it. But this time a child lay cradled in her womb, and the man behind her would soon be her husband.

Neither spoke, for words proved unnecessary. They belonged to this room, to their baby, to each other.

Colt's mouth brushed the side of her neck, and she turned to face him. Their lips met ever so gently. She all but melted, feeling seventeen once again and enamored of a kind-hearted cowboy. He held her close, then knelt to press a tender kiss upon her tummy. Melanie touched his hair and smiled. For a time they gazed at each other, sharing the moment. When he stood, they joined hands and walked quietly to the master bedroom.

The spacious suite benefited from Colt's Montana roots, boasting beamed ceilings and a stone hearth. A tall pine dresser displayed a set of wrought-iron candelabras. Beside them a bundle of sage burned in a small clay pot. The sweet earthy smell aroused Melanie's senses.

Colt's husky voice beckoned. "I want you to move in. To-night," he emphasized. "This is our house now."

She reclined on the four-poster bed. "Is that an order, Mr. Raintree?"

"Yes." He removed his shirt. "It is."

She watched him, enthralled by the power of his body, the broad expanse of his chest, slim line of his hips. Clad in unfastened jeans, he slid onto the bed, crawling toward her like a jungle cat—a sleek, sensual creature.

"I've missed touching you," he whispered, reaching for the buttons on her delicate cotton dress. Her feet and legs were already bare, and she longed to be naked. To feel his flesh against hers.

He undressed her slowly, taking care with each button. While he worked them free, she lowered her gaze to his open fly, to the shadow of dark hair and strain of his erection. He was perfect. And he was hers.

He lifted her dress, then sat on his heels to look at her. Pleasure shone in his eyes. Clearly he liked what he saw—a woman in a white lace bra and matching panties, her hair loose about her shoulders, her tummy swollen with his child. Just a little bit pregnant, she thought, but enough to make him proud of the change in her body.

Colt kissed her then, tongue to tongue—a moist, playful kiss that flared her passion. Within a heartbeat they shed the remainder of their clothes and she moved closer. He smiled and slipped his hand between her thighs.

Melanie abandoned herself to the sensations he incited and shifted her legs, inviting more of his touch. He continued the sensual pursuit, stroking her with a steady rhythm, spreading ripples of excitement through her veins.

He made a sound, a deep virile groan as she pressed him low in the belly and traced his erection with her thumb. They lay side by side, touching, kissing, generously giving pleasure, greedily taking it. And when she climaxed from his skillful manipulations, he watched her, his lips curving into a satisfied smile.

"You're beautiful," he said.

She skimmed his cheek, the smooth copper skin, rough masculine beard stubble. "You make me feel beautiful."

Their eyes met as he moved over her, eager yet gentle. She raised her hips to accept his penetration, ready to sheath the rigid length. He entered her easily, their hearts soaring in perfect harmony.

Melanie crooned his name and ran her hands through his hair. Long, lean, muscular Colt. Jungle-cat sensuality. He felt like a dark-eyed panther moving inside her, mating her for life, claiming her for his own. As she snaked her tongue out to taste the salty succulence of his skin, he shivered. Bewitched, she arched and purred. The scent of sage continued to drift through the air, melding with human arousal.

She wanted this joining to last forever, the swells and shudders, the tender, erotic feeling of being in love. Yet she wanted him to increase the tempo, to push faster, stronger, deeper.

He groaned and she caressed him. Everywhere. His face, his neck, each hardened nipple, the flat, rippling stomach. In turn, he kissed her, sending shocks of electricity through her core. And when she began to shake, Colt arched his back, grasped her hips, and thrust deeper, filling her with all he had to give. Love. And liquid fire.

Colt pricked his finger with the boutonniere and cursed. He'd never been so happy, yet so nervous in his life.

"Here, let me do it." Shorty pinned the white rose onto Colt's lapel and stepped back to study him. "You look fine. Real dapper."

"You think so?" He tugged on the tie. The men wore traditional black tuxedos. Colt preferred to keep the masculine attire as simple as possible. He wondered if his hair looked okay, but didn't ask. He had combed it away from his face and secured it into a tight ponytail.

"The house turned out festive," Shorty said, gazing around the room.

"Sure did." Vases of flowers graced the rustic interior, as did clusters of heart-shaped balloons. Pink and white streamers draped artfully from the wood beams. Everyone, including Glo-

ria's kids, had participated in decorating, adding their own creative touches. Shorty had helped Colt arrange the extra tables
and chairs, while the females fussed over the pastel splendor and
silver bells.

Shorty sniffed the air. "Something smells good."

Colt nodded. Two caterers, hard at work, made use of the
well-equipped kitchen. A prime rib dinner would be served in
the formal dining room, and soon, trays of hors d'oeuvres and
small baskets of candy would be scattered about.

Colt had arranged a limousine for the ladies and children, all
of whom, were thrilled about being chauffeured to the church.
Since Fred planned to drive himself over, Shorty and Colt decided to ride together.

Colt was glad to have Shorty take such an important role in
his wedding, and thought the gruff cowboy cleaned up nice. The
black tux suited him well. "You know, Shorty, you look pretty
good yourself. It does seem strange to see you without a hat,
though."

Shorty rubbed his head. "Yeah, feels odd, too." He reached
into his pocket and handed Colt a black leather strip with an
eagle feather and a strand of small silver beads attached. "This
belonged to Toby Raintree, your pa. He used to wear it in his
hair, and he gave it to your momma on the day your grandpa
run him off. Your ma was so young, and your grandpa wasn't
happy about a grown man courting his teenage daughter."

Colt listened intently as Shorty spoke about the father he had
never known. "Toby promised your grandpa he wouldn't come
back for your ma when she come of age, and he never did. Your
granddaddy didn't want her marrying some poor ranch hand, but
then again, he didn't know that cowboy had already made a
baby with her. Nobody did. Your ma didn't find out she was
carrying you until months after Toby was long gone."

"Anyway," Shorty continued, fingering the beads. "Your ma
gave this to me when she found out she was dying. She told
me to give it to you when you fell in love, to remember her and
your daddy by. Toby was a drifter and a bit on the wild side,
but she loved him."

Colt took the leather ornament and wiped away the moisture

lining his eyes, realizing how important his father's feather must have been to his mother. He studied the gift with respect, recognizing the marks of the gray eagle, one of the most revered animals in the Cheyenne culture. "Will you tie it on for me?"

Shorty fastened the leather around Colt's ponytail. "Looks good, son. Your momma would be proud."

"Thanks." The two men hugged. "I know my mom would have liked Melanie."

The older man nodded. "Melanie's a good girl, Colt. You take care of her."

"I will, Shorty. I promise." He smiled as he thought about his soon-to-be bride, knowing she would be at the church by now, preparing herself in the dressing room the chapel provided.

Melanie secured the last pin into her hair and gazed at her reflection. She had styled her hair into a loose topknot, just the way Colt had suggested. She knew he found the look appealing and especially liked the fiery tendrils that framed her face. Melanie smiled. He loved her, truly loved her. And he told her every day, but not just in words. Colt expressed his devotion through boyish winks, sensuous smiles and reverent touches. They had shared everything lately, including their most private thoughts. Each had explored the other's heart until the two life forces had no choice but to beat as one. And now they would become one in the eyes of the world. Dreams, she thought, do come true.

Gloria came up behind her, and the two women looked at each other in the mirror. "We are gorgeous, aren't we?"

Melanie laughed and glanced around the small room at all the ladies waiting to walk down the aisle. "Yes, we are."

Gloria and her daughters were dressed in pink chiffon and lace. Each had a crown of tiny flowers in her hair. Gloria's bouquet had been fashioned from pink and white roses, and the flower girls would be sprinkling pink and white petals down the aisle. Melanie was given long-stemmed roses to carry because Colt had suggested a bouquet as graceful as the lines of her body. The poetry in his words had warmed the woman in her.

"Are you nervous?" Gloria asked.

Melanie nodded. "It's a good kind of nervous, though."

Gloria reached into a slim gold box and removed a strand of pearls. "I want you to wear these, and then keep them to remember your family by." The other woman clasped the delicate pearls around her neck. They shone exquisitely with the silk dress. "My family is your family, Mel. We love you like you're one of our own."

"They're beautiful, thank you," Melanie said, knowing tears were just a heartbeat away. "And I love you, too. All of you."

As soon as Melanie's tears began to flow, Gloria produced an embroidered handkerchief and dabbed her cheeks. "Oh, goodness. Don't smear your mascara now. It's almost time."

The twin girls grinned at both women, then gasped when the music started. "Go on," their mother prodded, shooing them out the door. Gloria's older daughters followed the twins, starting their walk as bridesmaids.

Gloria picked up her bouquet. "I better get going so they can play your song."

When her song was played and the guests stood to receive her, Melanie accepted Shorty's arm and met Colt's smile with one of her own.

Colt nodded to Shorty, swept Melanie into a warm embrace and held her close. "I love you," he whispered.

"I love you, too," she responded, melting gloriously from his touch. Pure happiness spilled through her. For the rest of her life the sky would be bluer, the stars brighter, rain on her tongue fresher, the beat of her heart stronger. She would live each hour to the fullest and create beauty with the man she had never forgotten.

The groom spotted the bride's invitation from across the room and casually made his way over to her. He'd had no idea that he would have to spend most of his wedding reception mingling with the guests.

"Hi," he said, flashing her his most flirtatious smile. "My name's Colt."

She laughed and extended her hand. "Melanie."

He lifted her hand and brushed it with a gallant kiss. "Would you be interested in sleeping with me?"

She widened her eyes. "That's not what you're supposed to say to a girl you've just met."

"Oh, you're right." He cleared his throat and started over. "You are the most gorgeous creature I've ever seen. Do you want to paint my body, then make mad, passionate love?"

They hugged and laughed. "Everyone is here," she said. "Even Tiffany and JR."

"Yeah." Colt scanned the crowd for the eccentric California blonde. She had glided into the church wearing a silver jumpsuit, a white fringe jacket and the fanciest cowboy boots Colt had ever seen. "Can you believe she dressed that dog up for the occasion? Jeez, a bow tie and everything. I hope Sparky doesn't start asking for clothes. He likes JR. They've been playing together all evening."

Melanie leaned her head against her husband's shoulder. "Did you see the looks Shorty and Tiffany were exchanging?"

"No, but I can imagine. Talk about culture shock."

"Are you kidding? I think they're sweet on each other."

Colt grinned. "She's weird but she's good-looking. The old guy could do worse."

She nudged his ribs. "You're such a chauvinist."

"Yeah, aren't you glad you married me?" He looked around. "What do you say we slip out of here?"

"And go where?"

"Your former cabin."

She nibbled his ear. "You mean the honeymoon suite?"

"The very one."

They made their way to the back door and Colt scooped her into his arms, intending to carry his wife across the ranch and over the threshold. "Darlin'?"

"Hmm?"

"Would you rather go to the Chevy instead?"

She kicked off her shoes and kissed his teasing smile. "I'd go anywhere with you, cowboy. Absolutely anywhere."

Epilogue

Snow fell from the vast Montana sky the morning Andrew "Drew" Raintree was born. And now Colt stood, just hours later, cradling that new life in his arms. The infant, dressed in a pale blue sleeping gown and wrapped in a downy white blanket, drifted between wake and sleep, his eyes struggling to focus.

Colt glanced over at his wife and smiled. From the hospital bed, she watched him with a woman's adoration, but remained silent while he carried Drew toward the window. The view overlooked the small country town of Mountain Bluff, its simple buildings and quiet streets blanketed in snow. It was home, Colt thought, and the babe in his arms made it even more so. Meagan, too, had been born in Mountain Bluff, and it was there that she had been buried.

Colt's heart warmed as Drew made a soft cooing sound. He held the boy against his shoulder and inhaled the infant's sweet baby skin.

Meagan would have loved her brother. She would have marveled at each tiny finger and perfectly formed nail. She would have touched his soft rounded cheek and vowed to protect him forever. And she still would, he thought. Every night when baby Andrew dreamed, Meagan would be there, a loving guardian angel.

Colt stroked his son's head, and when Drew's hair tickled his fingers, he laughed. The boy looked so much like him with his bronze complexion and thatch of midnight hair, the child's familiar image stirred his pride.

Overwhelmed with joy, Colt turned back to his wife. Melanie had labored long and hard to give birth to his son, and he would be forever grateful. Although her hair fell about her shoulders in limp auburn strands and her eyes were dogged with pale shadows, he decided, at this very moment, Melanie Raintree was the most beautiful woman on earth.

She patted the empty space beside her. "I want to hold both of my men."

"Okay." He grinned at the thought and settled baby Drew into her waiting arms. After leaving his boots on the floor next to her slippers, Colt lowered himself to the bed, then snuggled beside her.

Drew curled his fingers around her gown and Melanie unbuttoned the front and brought his head to her breast. Immediately the boy rooted his tiny mouth upon the maternal offering. Melanie hummed a quiet lullaby and Colt closed his eyes and listened to the sound of family—a sound he would cherish forever.

*   *   *   *   *

Watch for Sheri WhiteFeather's next book, coming in February 2000 from Silhouette Desire.

THE F RTUNES OF TEXAS

*Membership in this family has
its privileges…and its price.
But what a fortune can't buy,
a true-bred Texas love is sure to bring!*

Coming in November 1999…

Expecting…
In Texas
by

MARIE FERRARELLA

Wrangler Cruz Perez's night of passion with Savannah Clark
had left the beauty pregnant with his child. Cruz's cowboy
code of honor demanded he do right by the expectant
mother, but could he convince Savannah—and himself—
that his offer of marriage was inspired by true love?

THE FORTUNES OF TEXAS continues with
A Willing Wife by Jackie Merritt,
available in December 1999 from
Silhouette Books.

Available at your favorite retail outlet.

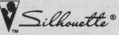

No one can anticipate the unexpected,
be it lust, love or larceny...

SOMETHING TO HIDE

**Two exciting
full-length novels by**

TESS
GERRITSEN

and

LYNN
ERICKSON

Intrigue and romance are combined in
this thrilling collection of heart-stopping
adventure with a guaranteed happy ending.

Available October 1999 at your favorite retail outlet.

HARLEQUIN®
Makes any time special ™

Visit us at www.romance.net

PSBR21099

SILHOUETTE® Desire®

COMING NEXT MONTH

#1249 HEART OF TEXAS—Mary Lynn Baxter
Man of the Month 10th Anniversary
Businessman Clark Garrison had come home to River Oaks for
one purpose—to make a profit. But that was before he met
Dr. Sara Wilson...and realized his profit would be her loss.
Would Sara still want to be his partner in life once the truth
was revealed?

#1250 SECRET AGENT DAD—Metsy Hingle
Texas Cattleman's Club
Widow Josie Walter had never wanted to get close to another
man again, but she couldn't help believing in happily-ever-after
when handsome amnesiac Blake Hunt landed on her doorstep—
with four-month-old twins. But once regained, would Blake's
memory include a knowledge of the love they'd shared?

#1251 THE BRIDE-IN-LAW—Dixie Browning
His father had eloped! And now Tucker Dennis was faced with
the bride's younger niece, Annie Summers. Annie only wanted
her aunt's happiness, but when she met Tucker, she couldn't help
but wonder if marrying him would make *her* dreams come true.

#1252 A DOCTOR IN HER STOCKING—Elizabeth Bevarly
From Here to Maternity
He had promised to do a good deed before the end of the day,
and Dr. Reed Atchinson had decided that helping pregnant
Mindy Harmon was going to be that good deed. The stubborn
beauty had refused his offer of a home for the holidays—but
would she refuse his heart?

#1253 THE DADDY SEARCH—Shawna Delacorte
Lexi Parker was determined to track down her nephew's father.
But the man her sister said was responsible was rancher
Nick Clayton—a man Lexi fell in love with at first sight. Would
Nick's passion for her disappear once he found out why she was
on his ranch?

#1254 SAIL AWAY—Kathleen Korbel
Piracy on the high seas left Ethan Campbell on the run—and in
the debt of his rescuer, Lilly Kokoa. But once—*if*—they survived,
would Ethan's passion for Lilly endure the test of time?